coyote morning

coyote
MORNING

a novel

Lisa Lenard-Cook

University of New Mexico Press
Albuquerque

10   09   08   07   06   05   04

1   2   3   4   5   6   7

Library of Congress Cataloging-in-Publication Data

Lenard-Cook, Lisa.
Coyote morning / Lisa Lenard-Cook.— 1st ed.
p.   cm.
ISBN 0-8263-3466-0 (pbk : alk. paper)
1. Human-animal relationships—Fiction. 2. Mothers
and daughters—Fiction. 3. Animals—Treatment—
Fiction. 4. Coyote—Control—Fiction. 5. Single
mothers—Fiction. 6. New Mexico—Fiction.
7. Coyote—Fiction. 8. Girls—Fiction.
I. Title.
PS3612.E52C695 2004
813'.6—dc22
2004005283

Printed and bound in the USA by Sheridan Inc.
Set in Janson 11.5/14.3
Design and composition: Robyn Mundy

*No tendency among humans is greater than to blame
others for what the blamers themselves do.*

—J. Frank Dobie

*The problem is the truth has become something that
doesn't interest people.*

—Elie Wiesel

coyote morning

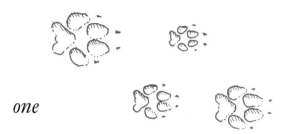

one

Coyote Facts

Identification: Coyotes (*Canis latrans*) weigh between 20 and 40 pounds. They resemble a small German shepherd with a slender muzzle and a bushy tail that is usually carried at a 45-degree angle. Coyotes are predominantly brownish gray in color with a light gray to cream colored belly. Colors vary from nearly black to red or white.

On that Monday morning in April, Alison Lomez watched through her kitchen window as her seven-year-old daughter Rachel shuffled to the end of their gravel driveway, where the school bus would stop for her. At first, Alison thought it was a dog that trotted up and sat down next to Rachel, a small yellow dog that reached to Rachel's chest. Dog and girl watched the empty road that wound down from the mesa. *Whose dog?* Alison thought, and then, *what kind?* and then, *coyote.* At this, the animal slowly turned its head, and looked Alison squarely in the eye. As Alison watched, Rachel bent to say something to the animal before resuming her vigil.

What Alison would come back to about that morning was the moment when she'd thought *coyote* and how the coyote had turned, as if it had heard. When the coyote looked at her, her mind decelerated, or so it felt, while her chest constricted around her heart until all that was left was a stone clutched in the center of her that she'd feel forever after. *Rachel,* she croaked, the name not really rising from her throat, the broken word like the panic of a dream, while all the time, the coyote just kept watching her, casually, over its shoulder. Then, suddenly, the bright yellow school bus was there, swallowing Rachel into its hydraulic maw before it resumed its crawl down the mesa.

The coyote sat a moment longer. Then it stood and trotted up the road in the direction from which the bus had come. Alison swallowed, finally, then focused her mind until the swallow circumvented her now-swollen heart and she could breathe again.

VALLE BOSQUE BEACON

To the editor:

That Natalie Harold who loves coyotes should come see what's left of my kids' rooster. He was their 4-H project, and he was a beauty, but that's not the point. The coyotes didn't even bother to swallow Banjo, they just killed him and then trotted away. For this village to allow coyotes to get away with wanton murders like this is a crime. What's left of my kids' rooster is here for Mrs. Harold to see. I hope she does.

Yours truly,

Kathy Crawford

Where Natalie Harold came from, the wildest thing she ever saw was the motion of an invisible bird in a tree. Everything was close there, close and grey, and so when she first saw the sky over the desert she knew it was the place she'd never even known to dream, and she knew she was home.

When Natalie was the first person to walk the ditch bank in the morning, as she was today, the S's of night lizards would draw her paths for her. Small catches of coyote fur might dandle from chamisa; small patches of rabbit fur below suggested a recent repast. This early, the sun had not yet crested Sandia Mountain to the east, the mountain that the Indians called Turtle Mountain not only because of its shape but also because of its seeming motion, and some mornings, the air might still tang from a late evening rain, the sand still clot with the last of its moisture.

As always, Natalie walked slowly and, like most Valle Bosqueleños, she carried a big stick. The stick was to ward off loose dogs. She walked slowly in case today was the day she would finally see a coyote, her long-held and most cherished dream.

Every morning for thirty years, through the chill winds of winter, the sharp bites of imperceptible spring gnats, the slow heat of summer, and the smoke-heavy air of autumn, Natalie had sought a glimpse of her elusive prey. All around her people saw coyotes daily. Some had been seen as they trotted along this very ditch bank. Some were spotted as they ran across the two-lane main road. Others had been simply sitting and howling in one of the few unclaimed fields of sage. And yet Natalie, whose passion for the coyote was matched only by her passion for this place she had grown to call home, had seen only their leavings: fur-wrapped pointed scat, digitigrade four-pronged tracks, a tuft of fur inadvertently left behind. She had heard them, yes; everyone in Valle Bosque had heard a coyote. But as many sunrises as she'd seen, the sighting of a coyote had eluded her.

The lightening sky alerted her to yet another sunrise, and Natalie turned east to see the outline of the mountain momentarily edged in gold. Watching the sun rise over that mountain was a reminder to her of the god in all things: the god in the mountain, the god in the sky, the god in the sun as it revealed itself, and finally the god in one's self and one's surroundings. In her years in Valle Bosque, Natalie had come to her own mode of prayer, a naming of what mattered, a cherishing of those words, and an effort at coexisting with those so named.

Home was a word that had meaning here, in a way Natalie had never understood in the place where she grew up. *Home* was understanding that people were never alone, that the world was as large as all who lived in it, and that all must live there, together.

Alison glanced at the house as she backed out of the drive, uncomfortably aware that because of the coyote it now felt less like home. She was late for work, late because instead of her morning run she'd called Animal Control and had gotten into one of those circuitous conversations that was possible only with employees whose lone job description seemed to be making it to their retirement and their pension.

She'd wanted to be calm when she called, so she'd first gone into the small bedroom she'd taken for her den to sit cross-legged on her yoga mat. Chris had used this room for a home office until he'd left, and even though they'd been separated for three months now, Alison still felt as if her presence there was illicit when she first entered the room. They'd moved to the upscale village only six months before, once Chris's growing ophthalmology practice had made it possible. Now Chris was living with his new young love in a hip Old Town condo, while Alison pretended she belonged in a place like Valle Bosque.

Alison settled into her cross-legged posture, and then, breathing, watched Sandia Mountain dissolve into morning, the way it did this time of year, which was spring. She watched the mountain and breathed deeply in and then deeply out, and as she breathed out she let her mantra syllable escape as well: *woe*, or *whoa*, or maybe simply *wo*.

Rachel, she thought as she inhaled. Her breath caught. She knew she wasn't going to relax.

Back in the kitchen, she pulled the phone book from the drawer and found the number in the blue government pages in the front. She was hyperventilating. *Breathe,* she told herself. *Breathe.* She dialed the number. She told the woman who answered that a coyote had been in her driveway, had waited for the school bus with her daughter. She heard the woman's sharp intake of breath.

How old?

How old? Alison echoed.

Your daughter. How old is your daughter?

Seven. Rachel's seven. Again, she heard the woman's breath catch and then release.

Hold on. I'll see if Ralph's in yet. The phone clicked into silence. Alison breathed some more. *In. Out. In. Out.*

Sandoval, said the male voice.

Alison thought the voice sounded suspicious. But why did she think this? She was reading into things again. It was one of the reasons Chris had left her, or so he had said. Mr. Sandoval, this is Alison Lomez. I live up in Mesa Playa. *Breathe.* This morning, while my daughter was waiting for the school bus— Alison told Mr. Sandoval her story. She heard him breathing nasally in the pauses where she too breathed, in and out.

They don't usually hurt kids, he said when she finished telling him.

Usually?

Usually, they eat cats and poodles and chickens and lambs, if they go for the domestic animals at all. Usually, there's plenty of rabbits and mice to go around.

So you're saying the coyote was not threatening my daughter.

I'm saying they eat small animals.

And would it consider my daughter a small animal?

Is she small?

She's seven.

She heard Mr. Sandoval's inhale-exhale while he considered this answer. I can't say I know the size of a seven-year-old girl, he said at last.

She's small, Alison said. She could hear the impatience creeping into her voice, the impatience she practiced so hard to erase.

Well, I don't know then, said Mr. Sandoval.

Is there something you can do? Alison asked.

That depends.

Depends on what?

If it threatened her. Did it threaten her?

It sat down next to her. It knew I was watching from the window. It turned. It watched me watching.

But it didn't threaten her.

It was there. That's a threat.

I'll put it in my log, Mr. Sandoval said.

Alison breathed. *In. Out.* Counted to ten. Thank you, she said. Then she hung up.

2003: Coyote Tracking Log

Date	Time	Location	Incident Reported
4/7/03	7:50 a.m.	Ms. Lomez—Mesa Playa	Coyote approached 7 yr girl

To the editor:

I was sorry to hear about Ms. Crawford's children's chicken. It must have been difficult for her children, and yet the fault is partly Ms. Crawford's, in not taking the measures necessary to ensure a coyote could not get into her pen. Research has shown that simply roofing one's chicken coop will keep coyotes out. Giving chickens the run of a place offers coyotes an all-too-easy free lunch. Coyotes are clever and adaptable animals who survive on the prey they catch and kill. Coyotes do not, however, know the difference between domestic animals and their natural wild prey, and as we encroach more and more on their habitat and so their natural prey, they will of course seek their sustenance wherever they may find it. Coyote education booklets are now available at the village offices. I've taken the liberty of placing one in Ms. Crawford's mailbox as well.

Sincerely,

Natalie Harold

To the editor:

That Harold woman doesn't even know a chicken from a rooster. Would she say the same thing if the coyote would of eaten one of Kathy Crawford's kids instead of one of their roosters? I hear that back east they use guns to shoot people *instead of coyotes. Maybe Mrs. Harold should go back there where she came from and leave us alone.*

Jim Curtis

When the wind blew from the north, planes leaving the Albuquerque Sunport took off directly overhead. Depending on the season, the coyotes that lived in the empty field behind Natalie's house would respond to the jets' roar. First, there would be high *yip-yip-yip* she'd come to recognize as the alpha female, then, if it were pup season, the still higher-pitched confusion of her latest brood. If he was around, the old alpha male would chime in next with his plaintive slow howl, and this year Natalie had recognized two distinct new voices nearby that she thought might be yearlings from last season's litter.

Lately, the dogs next door often barked first when they heard a plane overhead. It had started as an answer to the coyotes, but the dogs had learned which sounds set the coyotes off and anticipated them. The coyotes, if they were around, would respond whether there was jet noise or not. It was almost like a conversation sometimes, the alpha female's *yip-yip-yip* followed by the neighbor Border Collie's harried *woof-woof-woof* and then the Lab's low and slow: *Roof. Roof. Roof.* Natalie would sit on her *portal* and be tempted to join in. What would she sound like to them? she wondered. Would they recognize her voice as human and feel threatened, or maybe stop altogether? Would they appreciate that she only sought to understand, and let her sing along?

Natalie loved the sounds of the coyotes' voices, that each voice was separate and distinct. She loved the way their primeval chorus rose up to disappear into the indigo night sky that contained more stars than she'd ever imagined existed when she was a girl. She loved the moon-bright nights in winter that were like half-days, and she loved the summer silence left when the cicadas stopped their dentist-drill chorus on some pre-arranged signal. She even loved the hustle of wind that cha-cha'd the old elm branches to let them know it was spring, and the mnemonic smell as her neighbors burned those branches on early autumn mornings.

She'd heard the coyotes often in the winter, but now that it was spring she didn't hear them as frequently, even when the jets took off overhead. After so many years of listening, she understood that they'd return, that they were just getting their wandering legs back after a winter spent close to home. But she worried, too. She worried that maybe this time they wouldn't be back. Ralph Sandoval from Animal Control had told her he'd heard someone had shot a coyote over by the old camposanto, and she was afraid it was her alpha male, he of the plaintive slow howl. Now she sometimes strained to hear his voice calling from anywhere in the village or even beyond. She'd think of Shirley Booth then, in *Come Back, Little Sheba*, how she'd stand at her door in her curlers and robe and call that little dog that was never coming back, night after night. Natalie wondered if she was becoming a character like Booth's Lola, whose life had escaped out her rickety screen door in the one moment she'd let herself be distracted. Then she'd think she heard a high-pitched yipping, so far off she couldn't be sure, and she'd concentrate on listening as far into the night as her hearing could carry her.

Is he here? Rachel asked as soon as Alison turned into the driveway. Because it was a Monday, Alison had picked Rachel up after soccer practice instead of rushing home to meet the school bus at four, as she did every other day.

Who? Daddy? she answered. It's Monday, honey. You know Daddy comes on Friday. Alison waited for the garage door to finish rising and then pulled in.

Not *Daddy*. The *coyote*.

Alison decided to act as if it weren't a big deal. Maybe it wasn't. What did she know? Well, she thought, who *did* know? That woman, the one who wrote the letters to the paper, she answered herself. She tried to remember her name.

I haven't seen him, Alison said. Can you get your seat belt undone yourself? She reached into the back seat to help.

His name is Chris, Rachel said as she slid out of the car.

It is, is it? Alison tried not to attach any meaning to Rachel's naming a coyote after her father, but it wasn't going to work. She wondered what Chris was doing. She told herself she didn't care.

She held the door open and Rachel marched under

her arm into the laundry room, then turned to face her, hands on hips. Suzy Charles says you can't *have* a coyote.

I'm afraid she's right.

Why are you *afraid?* Of the *coyote?*

Alison dropped her purse and papers onto the washer and continued into the kitchen. Should we have spaghetti for dinner? Spaghetti and salad, how's that sound?

Well, *I'm* not afraid of the coyote. He's my *friend.* Rachel had acquired her new emphatic way of speaking in the second grade. She'd probably learned it from Suzy Charles. Now she eyed Alison a second longer before spinning on the heel of her Reebok with what must have been a satisfying squeak and then running to her room. The door closed behind her.

Alison got out a pot, filled it, and set it on to boil, then poured herself a glass of Merlot to fix a salad by. She wanted Rachel to be afraid of the coyote, but she didn't want her to know to be afraid. It seemed as if she had to file everything she wanted under something else. It seemed as if she had a surface life and an under-life, the latter teeming with things that dared not show their ugly little heads. Even her job was that way. A public information officer for a major construction project down in Albuquerque, Alison knew it was all in the phrasing—she refused to call it spin— in the way you arranged the words to reveal the meaning you wanted to show.

Alison's friend Molly wouldn't see it this way at all. Molly and Alison had first met as journalism majors at the University of New Mexico, and even though that seemed to be all they had in common, they'd formed an immediate and lasting bond. After they graduated, Molly had been hired by the best advertising agency in Albuquerque, where she wrote smart, funny copy that sounded exactly like Molly herself. Whenever Alison felt like a fraud—far more often than anyone other than Molly knew—she would ask herself, WWMD: What would Molly do?

Of course, one of the inevitable answers was that Molly would never have married Chris in the first place. Sometimes, Alison wondered why Molly put up with *her*, but the one time she'd asked, Molly had told Alison she was the best part of her. When Alison asked what she meant, Molly said, *Think* about it, Alison, in that way she had, and Alison never asked again.

Still, she had thought about it. And what Alison had ultimately realized was that while Molly didn't exactly need a friend, Alison was the kind of friend she could and would have. Alison and Molly shared a shorthand all their own, one marked by an offhand irony others often missed. Alison was someone who not only laughed at Molly's jokes, but could bandy a few of her own as well. These days, it was important for Alison to simply remember that Molly cared about her. Of that much, Alison was certain.

The phone rang, startling Alison back into her kitchen. In separate areas of the house, she and Rachel said hello at the same time.

Hi honey, said Chris. Alison knew he wasn't talking to her. She was about to hang up, then changed her mind. She covered the mouthpiece with her hand.

I have a coyote, Rachel told him.

Chris laughed. Oh you do, do you?

He has the same name as you.

Oh he does, does he?

He waits for the school bus with me.

Alison heard Chris's quick intake of breath. Is Mommy there? he said.

Mommy! Rachel's voice stereoed through the hall and the phone. Alison clicked the flash button.

Hi, she said. Hang up, Rache.

I want to say goodbye again after, Rachel informed her parents before dropping her phone into its base with a clatter.

What's this about a coyote?

Alison told him. She repeated her conversation with Ralph Sandoval.

Christ.

Alison waited without responding.

Maybe she should live with me.

In your apartment. In Old Town. With you and Fifi.

Didi.

I wonder what Didi would think about that.

Didi loves Rachel.

Alison waited.

I'll bring my shotgun over. You can lock it up in the cabinet in the garage.

Oh, that's a great idea, Chris. You know what a good shot I am.

What the fuck would you like me to do?

I didn't ask you to *do* anything. If I recall, *you* asked to talk to *me*.

There you go again, Chris said.

Alison heard the edge in his voice, and felt for a moment the same vertigo she had when he'd still lived here, that lightheaded mix of incaution and fear. But Chris wasn't here. He wouldn't hurt her. Alison closed her eyes and leaped. I don't know why you always— She stopped as Rachel came into the kitchen. You want to say goodbye to Daddy? She handed Rachel the phone.

Bye, Daddy. Love you, too. Rachel passed the handset back to her mother and Alison hung it up. She finished the long swallow left in her wineglass. The water on the stove hissed and boiled and Alison dropped the spaghetti into the pot.

Natalie was sitting in the dark when she heard the phone ring in the kitchen. She'd been sitting in the window seat before it got dark, and she hadn't moved once the light had leached from the sky. Nor did she switch on the kitchen light to answer the phone; she groped toward the sound until she found the handset, clicked it on, and said hello.

It was her brother Sherman, calling from Denver. Natalie carried the handset back to the dark living room, where she could look out toward where she knew the mountain was. She told Sherman about the letters in the village paper, the *Valle Bosque Beacon*. She told him she wasn't certain if she should be frightened or not.

I'll be there tomorrow, Sherman said. Natalie knew that in one way, it was a response to what she'd said. Still, she was surprised: As she had learned throughout their mostly separate adult lives, Sherman's visits occurred as preludes to whatever move was coming next. She'd thought Sherman had finally settled in Denver, in a way he hadn't in LA or Phoenix, or even in Manhattan, where they had grown up. She'd often hoped that by the time they were both in their fifties, Sherman would have found a place to call home, as she had, although it had recently occurred to her that it was possible that, unlike her, a home was not what he desired.

I don't need protection, she said, but she was glad he would be there. She and Sherman had always had a special bond. Maybe it was because Sherman had been born only thirteen months after her. Maybe it was because their parents had been much older than those of their friends. But sibling rivalry had never been an aspect of their relationship. Their parents had believed in them, trusted them, and left them to themselves.

Do you remember how it was when we were growing up? Natalie asked Sherman now.

Sherman laughed. I remember that you always had your nose in a book. Some things don't change, do they?

No, Natalie said. They don't. But I was thinking about Mother and Daddy. How they believed in us.

Are you okay, Nat? Are you sure you're not worried about the guy who wrote that letter to the editor?

I was just thinking how, while everyone wished for fairy tale parents, you and I understood that the parents we had were far better than any about whom we had read in the Brothers Grimm or Hans Christian Andersen.

Are you depressed? Sherman asked. Is that why you're thinking of Mother and Daddy?

I'm not depressed. I'm looking forward to your visit. I was thinking about how close we've always been. How close we are still. How, even though we're both solitary sorts, we know the other will be there, when we need him or her.

Sherman didn't respond immediately. Natalie tried to picture him in his condo in Denver, but it was a place she'd never been. She put him on a balcony, looking out across the city lights toward the Rockies. He wouldn't be able to see them any more clearly than she could see Sandia Mountain from where she was sitting in the dark, she thought.

I try to be there, Sherman said at last. I *know* you'll be there.

It's not like I need you, Natalie reminded him in her stern big sister voice.

Now Sherman laughed. No. It's not like you *need* anyone. Especially me.

But she did need him, Natalie thought. She might not need anyone else, but Sherman's existence was as essential to her as her dream of seeing a coyote. Natalie realized that Sherman was waiting for her to speak. I'll be here, she said. Then they said their goodbyes.

Alison never used to watch TV, but now she turned it on every night after she'd tucked Rachel in. She hated being alone. She'd never been alone in her life until now, and she felt her solitude as a hollowness that might envelop her until she herself ceased to exist.

Tonight she was watching a rerun of some made-for-TV movie she hadn't even considered watching the first time and didn't want to watch now, either. The girl who'd been in *Little House on the Prairie* was in it, but she wasn't a girl anymore, and one of the guys from *St. Elsewhere*, or maybe it was *Hill Street Blues*. Old TV stars never died; they just got older and made shitty movies.

Alison was drinking bourbon. This wasn't a good sign. She didn't even like bourbon, but she'd wanted something that tasted like how she felt and it was what she'd found when she opened the cupboard where Chris had kept the hard liquor. Wild Turkey. What a name for something you drank. Did it indicate how you'd feel after a couple, or how you felt before you began? She'd had a couple and she didn't feel wild; she felt even emptier than when she'd started.

She'd thought they'd been reasonably happy. Well, she amended, they'd been *mostly* happy. Or, she could say, *often* happy. Okay, *sometimes* happy. All right, she admitted it: Sometimes it had been worse than a made-for-TV movie.

But then Didi came along. She probably screwed like a wild turkey. Alison smiled at that, then stopped smiling. How did wild turkeys screw? Molly said when it came down to it, screwing was all men really cared about. Alison had never believed this, just as she'd never precisely believed a lot of what Molly said. If Molly was right, it meant Alison had to reexamine everything Molly had ever told her. That would take time: Molly said a lot. Alison decided to call her—it was only 8:30—but Molly's machine came on. Alison told it to tell Molly to call her, if it wasn't too late, and then she hung up and set the phone on the table next to the book she was trying to read when she remembered. *Own Your Own Life*, it was called. Each of the 365 chapters was one page long. Alison kept getting behind.

She flipped the book open to where she'd stuck a receipt from Target and read. *Other people can't make you angry*, said the book. *Only* you *can make you angry*. Alison closed the book and set it back on the table, then poured a little more bourbon over what was left of the ice and took another sip. It didn't get any better the more you drank, that was for sure. When the phone rang, she almost dropped the glass.

I was in the bathroom, Molly said. How *are* you?

I are drinking bourbon. Wild Turkey, to be precise.

Ugh. You should try Scotch. A good single-malt. If you're going to become a lush, at least be classy about it.

I'm not going to become a lush. I just needed a drink.

Uh-huh. Molly didn't go on.

How come you're not talking? I called you because you always talk. I wanted to hear someone besides the TV talk.

Uh-oh.

What's that mean?

Just what it sounds like. You want me to come over? You know my toothbrush is always ready in my purse.

I didn't think that was for me.

It's not, but I'll make an exception. And I'll stop and buy some decent Scotch. I don't want it getting around that my best friend gets drunk on Wild Turkey.

Am I your best friend?

I'll be right over. The phone clicked off. Alison set the handset next to the bottle and picked up the glass again, then instead of drinking watched the Little House girl melt into a kiss that would have made Michael Landon turn over in his grave.

Then Molly was shaking her shoulder. You're one cheap date, she said, setting a bottle-shaped bag on the table amid the book, phone, and empty glass. Molly's hair was a new shade of red, somewhere between plum and prune.

I like your hair, Alison said.

Alison, you're lying. I've never known anyone who lied as much as you do.

I do not. Alison was wounded. I am wounded, she said.

And you lie worst to yourself. Christ. I don't know why I put up with you.

Alison felt herself beginning to cry.

Oh *shit*, Alison. The guy *is not worth it*. The guy is an *asshole*. Molly sat down on the arm of Alison's chair and hugged her. The guy is *history*, Alison. Molly pulled back. What's so funny?

The way you're *talking*. The way *Rachel* does. So *emphatically*.

Great minds. Molly got up and took the bottle from the bag. Glenlivet, she said. I only hope you can appreciate it in your depleted state. She went into the kitchen for ice and fresh glasses, then returned, carefully poured, and handed Alison a glass. To great Scotch, she said.

Here, here, said Alison. Or was it hear, hear? She giggled.

Molly arranged herself on the sofa, moving pillows until both she and the couch looked comfortable. What's really eating you?

Alison looked at the television, but Molly must have switched it off. How come you turned off the TV?

Alison.

There was a coyote. Alison talked in a rush, so she wouldn't leave anything out. Rachel was waiting for the school bus and a coyote came and sat down beside her. And when I called Animal Control, the guy acted like it was no big deal. Now Rachel wants to keep it. She named it Chris.

She told Chris about it and Chris wants me to take his shotgun and keep it in the garage. Is everybody crazy, Molly? Or is it just me?

A coyote? You sure?

I'm sure.

Molly finished her drink and got up to pour another then settled into her pillow nest again. Are they dangerous?

It *felt* dangerous. But I don't know. I just keep thinking about how it looked at me, over its shoulder, like it was the one in control and I was like, I don't know, I was just this *person*.

I think that's called anthropomorphism.

Molly.

You're talking about a coyote, Alison, not something in a cartoon, for chrissake.

Alison sipped her Scotch. Molly was right; it was better than the bourbon. But she was tired of drinking now and set the glass on the table next to her. I used to be the one in control, she said.

No one's in control, Alison. We only think we are. Life just keeps on rolling along with us or without us.

That's comforting.

No, I mean it. What do you think? That something you did differently would have kept Chris from getting the hots for Didi?

Maybe.

You don't think that.

How do you know what I think?

Because I *know* you, Alison. You know Chris and Didi had nothing to do with you. You were a casualty, but you weren't a cause.

Alison thought about that. There were things that Molly didn't know, of course, that only Alison and Chris knew, that she'd never tell anyone else, not even Molly. But Rachel knew. And in the end, she'd be the one most hurt. Rachel's a casualty, too, Alison told Molly.

Yes, and Chris is a shit for that, but there you go.

I always figured guys fell for younger women when they were older. Mid-life crisis and all that. Not when they were thirty-five, you know?

So much for broad generalization. Molly stretched and yawned. You want me to sleep on the couch?

Alison nodded, then got up for sheets and a comforter. It occurred to her that Molly was her comforter. She was going to tell her so, but by the time she got back to the living room, she'd forgotten. Instead, they tucked the sheets into the couch silently. Then Molly gave her a tight hug and pushed her off to her room. Alison didn't remember getting into bed, but she did.

Did you get a *dog*? says Suzy Charles. Rachel doesn't know what she means when she says that, so she asks her, What do you mean? Suzy says, I saw you waiting for the school bus with your dog, so then Rachel says, That wasn't a dog that was *my coyote*, and then she laughs because she *wants* it to be her coyote. Suzy Charles laughs too and Rachel decides she can be her friend today. His name is Chris, Rachel says. No, Suzy says, that's your *daddy's* name, and Rachel decides she's not her friend today anymore and maybe not tomorrow, either.

When Rachel says her prayers she says God bless the coyote and she hears Mommy make that noise like she does when she doesn't like something so Rachel says God bless *Chris my coyote* to see if Mommy is looking at her but if she is, she is pretending she isn't which is what she does all the time now that Daddy doesn't live with Rachel and her anymore. Daddy lives with Didi. Didi has hair that looks hard not like hair at all and Rachel wants to touch it but she doesn't because— well, just because. God bless Didi's *hair*, Rachel says, and then she says amen and looks at Mommy. Amen, Mommy says. Good night sleep tight don't let the bedbugs bite. Mommy kisses Rachel's head and then makes the light quiet like nighttime so then Rachel can go to sleep.

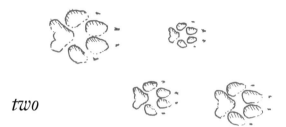

two

Coyote Facts

Food Source: Coyotes are opportunistic when it comes to getting their food. They seek out the easiest way to secure a meal. Coyotes feed on a wide range of animals such as rabbits, various rodents, small livestock and domestic pets like cats and dogs. Assorted fowl are also easy prey such as chickens, geese, ducks, turkeys and other birds. In addition, coyotes eat fruits such as grapes and apples, berries and vegetables.

To the editor:

In light of Ms. Crawford's and Mr. Curtis's recent letters, I would like to remind Valle Bosque Beacon *readers that coyotes do not "attack" at all. When they are hungry, they forage for, and find, a meal. Their only casualties are small animals. While I am sure it was frightening for Ms. Crawford's children to discover their dead rooster, I can assure her that it is highly unlikely the coyote would hurt the children themselves. If she would like to call me to discuss this, my phone number is in the directory.*

Sincerely,

Natalie Harold

The phone rang early, before 7 a.m., but Natalie was already up, getting ready for her walk. The sound set off a spike of worry: Had something happened to Sherman? Or to her ex-husband Keith? Despite her best effort to mask it, her voice when she answered betrayed her concern.

Did I wake you up? the male caller asked.

Who is this? Now Natalie worried for a different reason.

The caller barked a laugh. Let's start over, he said. This is Ralph Sandoval. I wanted to tell you that Frank asked me to set out some traps. For the coyotes.

The second-in-command of the village's two-man animal control operation, Ralph Sandoval had often shared information like this with Natalie in the past. It was he who passed the tracking logs on to her, he who had told her that the old alpha male might have been shot. But he had never called her before.

Natalie was cautious in her dealings with Ralph Sandoval. For one thing, she wasn't quite certain where his sympathies lay, although she suspected they were with the coyote, or he wouldn't bother keeping her informed. It was also because she knew Frank Sebold was far less charitably disposed toward her that she was careful with Ralph.

But she also knew that Ralph didn't mind long pauses in conversation while she thought over what he'd said. Sometimes the pauses were hers, sometimes his. Now she considered the information he'd just passed on. Can you tell me where? she asked him.

Ralph's pause suggested that the question had to go to some central location to find an answer and then bring it back. Natalie didn't mind, because what happened in his pauses often brought back answers she never expected. This time was no exception. You want to go with me? Ralph said. When I set one out?

Could I? Natalie wondered what Frank Sebold would think about that. Not only was Frank Sebold not a big fan of coyotes, he wasn't a big fan of hers. He wouldn't be pleased if he knew Natalie had accompanied Ralph on this mission.

Ralph paused again. Natalie waited. I could pick you up, he said. On a corner. When you're out walking like you do. I could pick you up around ten. Where your road ends at the ditch bank.

All right, she said. She wanted to say thank you, but she didn't. She knew that Ralph picking her up along the ditch bank would look like serendipity rather than something Ralph and Natalie had planned.

When she'd hung up, Natalie decided that rather than take two walks, she'd postpone her morning trek until she left to meet Ralph. She refrigerated the water bottle she'd been filling when the phone rang and made a pot of coffee instead.

It was after seven when Alison opened her eyes to squint at the alarm clock next to her bed, and when she saw the time, she bolted upright, a movement that generated a wave of vertigo so dizzying that she lay back down. She couldn't call in sick, she thought. Besides, a hangover was just reward for how much she'd drunk the night before.

Alison opened her eyes again, more slowly. The sun had risen well above the crest of the mountain. The school bus would be coming. She needed to check on Rachel. She thought of the coyote. She swung her feet off the bed, waited till the dizziness subsided, then padded into the bathroom.

When she got to the kitchen a few minutes later, Alison found an already-dressed Rachel carrying on an animated conversation with Molly. Cheerios decorated the tabletop around Rachel's bowl and Alison focused on the pattern they created.

I dressed myself, said Rachel.

Alison pulled out her chair and sat down, then took a closer look at what her daughter was wearing. The pink Oshkosh overalls, a size too small, over a lime and purple sweater that Alison knew had a gaping hole in the elbow. One yellow sock with orange ducks, one red with grey monkeys. Alison felt Molly looking at her and turned. Molly delivered a quick wink.

She has a future in fashion design, Molly said. She herself was wearing a sweatshirt Chris must have left behind. *Beep-beep*, it said above the Roadrunner's head. Alison thought of the coyote again, and rose to look out the kitchen window. The road that ribboned down the mesa was empty.

You made coffee, she said to Molly.

And Cheerios, Molly said.

Molly says she'll fix my hair, said Rachel.

Alison checked the time on the stove. Then you'd better get cracking, she said.

Rachel jumped up and pulled Molly from her chair. Will you do a Frenched braid? she asked.

I will do two Frenched braids, Molly told her. Coffee, she added to Alison over her shoulder. Black. It will help. Promise.

Alone in her kitchen, Alison obeyed, sipping coffee while continuing her surveillance through the window. Wile E. Coyote, she thought. No. She'd resist naming him, or her. She wouldn't name the coyote, and she wouldn't make a joke of it. It wasn't funny.

Rachel paraded into the kitchen, turning her head from side to side so Alison could see both of her French braids.

It's how you tell the pligs in Utah, Molly said, following Rachel back into the kitchen.

The what?

The pligs. The polygamists. Molly had been raised Mormon. Alison usually forgot, until Molly said something like this to remind her.

I thought there weren't any more polygamists, Alison said.

Yeah, said Molly. I forgot. Alison felt herself becoming annoyed. Maybe Molly first thing in the morning wasn't a good idea. Maybe it was why none of Molly's many boyfriends had lasted very long. As if Alison had done any better. *Don't go there*, she warned herself.

Rachel had her jacket on, and was closing the lid of her Barney lunchbox. What's in your lunchbox? Alison asked her, reaching. Rachel pulled it away.

I made her lunch, Molly said, winking again, this time at Rachel. Alison pictured gummy bears, Cheerios, Chips Ahoy, and Hershey's kisses crowding for space. I am a horrible mother, she thought. She poured herself another cup of coffee.

Who loves you? Rachel asked her. It was their morning ritual.

Rachel loves me, said Alison the horrible mother. Who loves you?

Mommy and Daddy, and my coyote and Molly, Rachel said. The latter two were new additions.

My new beau, said Molly. It took Alison a moment to realize she meant the coyote.

I love you best, Alison told Rachel, running her hand along one French braid.

No, said Rachel. I love you best. Alison felt tears beginning and took a sip of coffee to stop them. Then she leaned down and kissed the top of her daughter's head.

Once Rachel had slipped out the door, Alison resumed her post at the kitchen window. No coyote joined Rachel this morning, but Alison watched the school bus inch down the mesa long after it had picked Rachel up.

When she turned, she saw Molly watching her. Molly

had changed into her running clothes. Alison felt a wave of dizziness.

Figured I'd start without you, Molly said.

You can finish without me, too, said Alison. She put her hand to her head. You know any sure-fire cure for this?

Don't drink, Molly said.

Thanks a lot, said Alison. But she knew Molly was right. My head feels like it's split in two, she told her.

And that's something new? Molly asked. She had moved toward the back door and begun her pre-run stretches.

Alison laughed. It hurt, but she couldn't help it. What would I do without you? she said. You're exactly right. It's a physical manifestation of my mental bifurcation.

Molly placed her left foot on the door frame and then stretched her right arm toward it. In other words, she said, you feel like shit.

This was why Molly wrote clever ad copy while she wrote press releases for a construction project, Alison thought. She watched Molly switch legs, stretch her left arm toward her elevated right foot. She'd never be like Molly, she thought. She wasn't certain if the knowledge made her happy or sad.

When she was finished stretching, Molly turned toward her. You sure you don't want to come? she asked. Might make you feel better. I can wait while you change.

Alison shook her head and the dizziness returned. No, she said. You go. I deserve to be punished for drinking that much.

You're such a *Catholic*, Molly said with a smile. Then

she left. Alison hadn't been to church in years, but she knew what Molly meant. Through the window, she watched Molly shrink smaller and smaller as she ran up the mesa. Maybe Molly would see the coyote, Alison thought. Her new beau, she'd called it. Except that a coyote would never catch Molly. No one could catch Molly. Alison knew to not even try.

Sherman would be arriving sometime in the afternoon, so Natalie had to assume he had already left Denver. She was pleased there was a clear blue sky for his drive. She hoped the wind didn't pick up in the afternoon, as it often did in April.

Natalie couldn't imagine doing what Sherman did—hopping in his car to drive on the interstate at seventy-five miles per hour. Unlike Natalie, Sherman was a relaxed driver. Of course, neither one of them had learned to drive until they'd been grown. But not until she left Manhattan did Natalie realize how anomalous this was in the rest of the country.

As much as she loved New Mexico, Natalie had found herself thinking of Manhattan and their childhood more and more often. Their mother had been a writer, a fairly well-known one: If Natalie mentioned her name in certain circles, it set off a frisson of recognition. Their father had been the managing partner of a prosperous law firm that specialized in discreet management of property and money for wealthy New Yorkers. Neither had planned for nor expected children, but in their middle age, there the children were. Our little gifts, their mother called them. There was no reason for Natalie and Sherman to be skeptical of their mother's expression.

Natalie had wanted to be a writer, too, but unlike their mother, who wrote witty and literate nonfiction portraits about witty and literate subjects, Natalie was drawn to poetry. As being a poet and making a living were mutually exclusive, she taught school in the years immediately following her graduation from Vassar, until she met Keith Harold. She'd moved to New Mexico with him more than thirty years before when he was offered a surgical residency at UNM, and although they'd parted ways shortly after their arrival, she'd never thought of returning to New York.

She hadn't written a poem in nearly as many years. Like that of many young poets, her work had been largely self-reflective, and as she outgrew it, she hadn't sought to discover a new poetry to replace it. When first their father and then their mother died, Natalie and Sherman had inherited trusts that provided enough for each to live on.

But while her path could hardly be called exemplary, Natalie thought, Sherman's was still less focused. No. She was being kind. Sherman had no focus. Sherman flitted, from passion to passion, from job to job, and from woman to woman. He'd attended six different colleges but never completed a degree. He'd been, variously, a salesman of time-share condominiums in Scottsdale, a bartender at a resort in Antigua, an A&R man for a record label in Hollywood, and a stereo salesman in Reno. Most recently, he and a friend had received venture capital funding for a start-up Internet business. Natalie had never understood precisely what the business would do, and Sherman had never tried very hard to explain. In a recent e-mail, Sherman had said, among other things, that this venture had ceased to exist. Natalie had been momentarily relieved she hadn't invested in it, then was sorry to have felt such a thing at all, however fleetingly. Sherman had long since exhausted his half of their trust. It was hard for Natalie to not share hers.

Natalie went to the linen closet and got out the sheets for the guest-room bed. Through the window, she could see how the elm buds were eliding toward small pale green leaves, and she wished she were outside. Only then did she remember that Ralph Sandoval had said he'd pick her up on the ditch bank around 10. As it was 9:45, she left the bed unfinished and hurried to gather her jacket and bottle of water.

Despite four Advil, Alison's headache persisted well into midmorning. With every stab of pain, she blamed Chris, even though she knew the headache was her own stupid fault. It didn't help that she had arrived to a crisis at work, a fatal accident on the interstate the night before that might have been due to improper signage by her company's work crew.

Victor Serna, the project manager, didn't want to talk about it, but Alison needed a statement she could release to the press. As the division manager was vacationing in Hawaii, his input wasn't a possibility, and the higher-ups would plead ignorance, which was true in more ways than that in which they meant it. Victor was it, and Victor wasn't talking.

The first time Alison had tried to get a statement from him, Victor shut the door that separated his office from the rest of the office trailer in her face. Victor, Alison said to the door. Either you give me a statement or I put words in your mouth. When Victor didn't answer, Alison studied the peeling white veneer of the aluminum door, the dark smudges of Victor's fingerprints around the doorknob. She thought of how Chris would react, far less quietly. I'll come back in half an hour, she said to Victor's door. There was still no response.

Back at her desk, Alison stared at her computer screen. Pain arced from ear to ear in periodic bursts. Alison found herself thinking about Chris, about how angry he would get, not just at something she'd said, but sometimes, seemingly, for no reason at all.

Chris hadn't been physically violent, at least not often. His anger more often took the form of verbal smacks, and over the years Alison had learned to return his volleys. In fact, Alison had learned what would set him off so well that sometimes she'd say something just to watch him smash his serve. Her conversation through the door with Victor had reminded her of a time when she and Chris had first been married, before she'd learned to how to play the game.

They'd still been living at her parents' then. Alison was pregnant with the baby she lost shortly afterward, and she'd been lying on her bed with the door closed, fighting off both waves of nausea and a growing dread that something was wrong with the fetus she carried. She never knew how she'd known, but less than a week later that dread proved prescient.

Chris got home from work before her parents. He was

putting himself through medical school with a patchwork of jobs. Alison worked, too, as the receptionist for a marketing firm (it was where she'd gotten her start in public relations) but had called in sick when she'd been unable to rise from her bed that morning.

Alison didn't know why she'd locked the door after her last trip to the bathroom, but she had. She heard Chris come into the house, heard his footfalls through the kitchen, heard him stop outside the bedroom and then turn the door handle. The locked door didn't open.

Alison? You in there?

Alison didn't answer.

Alison? Let me in.

I'm sick, Chris. I can't get up.

Alison heard the door rattle as Chris tried to force it open. Open the goddamned door, Alison.

Please, Chris, said Alison. Go away.

Chris burst through the door in a splinter of sound and wood. On the bed, Alison curled fetally to protect herself. She'd never seen him like this before, but she knew from her friends what men were capable of. Don't, she said.

Chris stood over her, fists clenched. Don't what? he asked. The odd smile on his face was new then. It was only later that it became familiar.

Don't. Just don't.

Chris looked at her, head to toe and back again, finally stopping at the burgeoning belly she protected with her arms. Then he began to laugh. You lazy slut, he said. You make me sick. Without another word, he turned and left. Alison heard his truck start in the driveway and then squeal away. For a long time afterward, she'd lain there without moving. She hadn't cried. But she had told the baby that maybe coming into this world wasn't such a good idea after all. How could she have known?

Alison felt the trailer tremble as Victor prepared to exit his office and wiped away the tears she could feel starting. After a year of sharing this trailer with Victor, as well as the project engineer, job secretary, and assorted foremen and superintendents, Alison had unconsciously learned each person's particular effect on the shaky structure of their temporary quarters. Should she post herself by his door, or wait for him to come to her desk? Another stab of pain shot from temple to temple. She opted to wait.

Victor opened his door, scowled in her direction, then followed his scowl to her desk. Type this, he said. Alison shifted to her keyboard, ready to record his words. High Mesa Construction regrets the accident on I-40 early this morning but is in no way responsible for its occurrence, Victor dictated in his usual monotone.

That's it? Alison asked when she stopped typing.

What else you want? Victor asked.

Alison could tell by his voice that he wasn't angry with her anymore. Do you know what happened? she asked him.

Wind knocked over the last sign before the merge. But there were plenty of others before that one. Guy was probably going too fast to see any of 'em. Or, he didn't give a shit, thought he could make it. Didn't figure on an equally stupid guy in the lane next to him playing chicken. Who knows? Maybe he was pissed at his wife. Maybe his wife was pissed at him.

Victor's eyes challenged Alison to respond. Instead, she picked up the police report from her desk and read it again.

She could make it all fit together now, she thought. Okay, she told Victor. I can take it from here.

Victor turned and headed for the trailer's exit, then stopped. Thanks, Alison, he said without turning. You do good work.

Give me a raise, Alison said. Victor laughed, one quick syllable, before he went out the door. Alison exhaled, long and slow.

Nice try, Sally said. She was rearranging the papers that Victor's exit had scattered across her desk, and now she set her nameplate atop them, *Sally Montoya* embossed white on brown. Alison idly adjusted her own nameplate. *Alison Lomez*, it read. I should change it back, she thought. *Alison Reyes*. Her head stabbed.

Do you have another Advil? she asked Sally.

You still got that headache, si? Try some more coffee first.

Alison's nose twitched involuntarily. I couldn't drink another cup of coffee if it were the last liquid on earth.

I wouldn't want that cup either, Sally said. She opened her desk drawer and extracted a bottle of pills, then got up and set it on Alison's desk. Keep it till I need it, she said. My day will come.

Alison took two more Advil and slid the bottle into her own desk. Never again, she said. Sally, on her way back to her desk to answer the once-again ringing phone, laughed.

Alison considered Victor's statement on her computer monitor for a few moments, then began typing. When she was finished, she reread what she'd written, changed a few words, then saved and closed the document and opened her e-mail program, where she retrieved the document and sent it to everyone in her press release directory. She knew reporters would begin calling in the next five minutes, but there was time for a quick breath of mid-city air before they did. I'm going outside for a few, she told Sally. Let me know when the calls start.

Natalie walked as fast as she could, but Ralph Sandoval was already out of his truck when she got to the ditch bank, squatting next to some scat in the dried weeds that lined the canal. Coyote? Natalie asked, coming up next to him. Ralph shifted so she could see for herself.

Natalie kneeled as best she could, and watched as Ralph used a stick to separate one piece of scat from the others. Dark brown, grey-furred, and pointed at both ends, it wasn't yet dry. Looks like we just missed him, Ralph said. He stood up. Natalie rose less easily and began to follow him to his truck. When Ralph stopped to look over his shoulder, Natalie stopped and looked, too. There was nothing behind them.

Frank gave me a shoot-to-kill order, Ralph said. He hadn't started walking again, and now he was watching Natalie's face for a reaction. She considered how best to respond. Natalie didn't put coyotes ahead of people, though she'd been accused of it. But she didn't put people ahead of coyotes, either. She didn't want the coyote going the way of the Mexican Wolf because of misplaced human chauvinism. The coyotes had lived in Valle Bosque long before Anglos arrived. They were already there when the Hispanics had come 400 years ago, and were likely there even before the Indians, who called the coyote God's dog, and were the only population who seemed to understand the pragmatism of coexistence.

The pragmatism of coexistence, Natalie thought. She'd try to remember the phrase till she got home and could write it down. But here on the ditch bank, Ralph was still waiting for her response. Will you? she asked him. Shoot to kill?

If I have to, he said. He didn't look happy about it.

Once he'd started the truck, Ralph seemed more at ease. I was in Nam, he said, shifting into first. Natalie knew it wasn't the non sequitur it seemed. Rather than respond, she watched in the side mirror as the road behind them disappeared in a cloud of brown dust.

We'd shoot pigs, sometimes, Ralph went on. Vietnamese pigs? They're real smart. Some people have 'em as pets now. Say they're smarter 'n dogs. He slowed the truck as they approached one of the feeder roads that crossed the canal, waited for an SUV to pass, and then continued along the right-of-way.

It wasn't just the way the one you shot squealed, Ralph said. It was the way his family would, too. Like they cared about each other.

You can't really afford to romanticize animals in your job, Natalie said. She was careful not to look at him.

You mean think that animals feel things like we do? Yeah, I know. But you know why I took this job? 'Cause I love animals. I really do.

Natalie wasn't sure if Ralph was testing her in some way. But why would Ralph do such a thing? Ralph was what Sherman used to call a WYSIWYG guy. It was an early computer term: What you see is what you get. No hidden agendas. No layers of meaning. Sherman didn't mean it to be a compliment, but Natalie thought there were far worse qualities to which one could aspire.

Ralph braked suddenly and Natalie caught a glimpse of movement in the scrub that sloped down the side of the road away from the ditch. Was that a coyote? she asked him. They'd reached the wire enclosure that fenced a construction yard where an ever-fluid cast of illegal immigrants made adobes by hand.

Think so, Ralph said. He shut off the truck, then draped his arms over the steering wheel and leaned on them. In the side mirror, Natalie saw the dust behind them slowly settle back to the ground. She cranked down her window. Ralph's was already open.

From somewhere near the *iglesia vieja*, a peacock called its eerily human hello and another answered. A half mile away on the two-lane main road through the village, a truck downshifted with a deep groan. As these and other distant sounds receded, Natalie became aware of the quiet, and then of the sounds within the quiet—the soft rustle of light wind through still-dry brush; the scratching scurry of a small rodent's feet; the crackle of an unfallen leaf as a bird shifted in an old cottonwood.

This is as good a place as any, Ralph said. You want to watch? Without waiting for an answer, he climbed out and flipped open the toolbox mounted across the pickup bed. Natalie heard clanking sounds behind her.

How far could she take this commitment? she wondered. Could she bring herself to watch a trap being set? Could she come back to see a coyote who had wandered into it?

Ralph was standing outside her window. Dangling from one hand was a wire cage. In the other he held a shovel. Well? he said.

Natalie looked at the cage. It was the size of two milk crates and built in a similar fashion. What's the cage for? she asked him.

Ralph laughed. Natalie hadn't heard him laugh often, and it was a surprising sound, a low chuckle with genuine humor behind it. It's not a cage, he said. This is the trap.

Natalie had pictured corrugated iron jaws. She'd imagined them snapping shut on a coyote's foot, and she'd even visualized a coyote gnawing off its own leg to escape. She'd imagined every horror possible, but it hadn't occurred to her that Frank Sebold would sanction the use of a humane trap.

She climbed out of the truck. Yes, she said. Show me how you do this. Then she watched as Ralph cleared the brush and debris, dug a hole for the trap, rigged up the door, and arranged the brush so that the trap blended into its landscape.

Wait here, Ralph said when he'd finished. I got one more thing to add. Natalie watched him return to the truck, open the passenger door, then lift the lid of the cooler that sat on the center hump in front of the gearshift.

As he walked back toward her, Natalie saw Ralph extract a hamburger from a zippered Baggie. Nina made it, he said. Nina, Natalie knew, was Ralph's wife. Natalie watched him set the meat carefully at the far end of the buried cage.

That's that, he said, standing back to see if they could detect the cage's presence. They couldn't. Natalie was excited. She thought perhaps a coyote wouldn't either. She thought perhaps she'd finally get to meet a coyote face to face. If so, perhaps she'd find out if everything her heart told her were true, if coyotes operated, as people did, because of love, need, and desire.

2003: Coyote Tracking Log

Date	Time	Location	Incident Reported
4/8/03	11:00 a.m.	ditch bank by adobe yard	set humane trap

To the editor:

I've been reading about the lively coyote debate here in Valle Bosque with a great deal of interest. It seems to me it comes down to one side saying that the coyotes were here first, and the other side saying that domesticated life has more value than wildlife. As any Native American will tell you, neither side is right: The Native Americans were here first, and all life is sacred.

Peace,

Redfern Goldstein

Alison barely beat the school bus home. She hurried out the garage door to meet Rachel halfway up the driveway. How was school? she asked.

Fine, said Rachel. She kept walking toward the house and Alison fell into step with her. Alison was used to these one-word starts to their conversations.

What did you do today? she asked.

We walked along the *bosque?* Over by the *river?* And Mommy, you know who we *saw?* We saw *Chris!*

Alison held the door between the garage and the laundry room open and Rachel ducked under her arm. The coyote, Alison said, doing her best to sound neutral.

My coyote, Rachel corrected her.

How do you know it was your— how do you know it was Chris?

Because he *smiled* at me. Suzy *Charles* saw. *Everybody* saw.

Alison set down her purse and continued into the kitchen, where she opened the refrigerator and got out a box of juice and some carrot sticks. Did Ms. Turner see?

Rachel scowled. Uh-uh. She became suddenly and noticeably silent.

Did something happen, Rachel? Alison jabbed the pointed end of the straw into the cardboard container and set it on the table. Rachel sat down and pulled it toward her and drank. Rache?

I'm *drinking*.

Did Ms. Turner say something? Alison persisted.

Rachel pushed the carton away from her so fast it tipped. Alison dove for it and tilted it upright again. When she looked at Rachel, Alison saw that she had begun to cry. She kneeled next to Rachel's chair and brushed the tears away with her fingers. Tell me, Swee'pea. What did Ms. Turner say?

Rachel slapped Alison's hand away. It's all *your* fault, she said, glaring at Alison in a new way.

I need to be careful, Alison thought. She stood and retreated to her own chair and sat down. What's all my fault? she asked.

That I'm a *liar*.

Alison felt the same stone in her midsection she'd felt the day before when she'd first spotted the coyote. You're not a liar, she said first. Then, Why is it my fault? And then, Who said you're a liar? For just a moment, she felt seven years old, too.

Ms. Turner said. Rachel sniffled.

Why did Ms. Turner say that you're a liar?

Because *she* didn't see Chris. He hided from her.

Hid. He hid from her.

Yes. So she wouldn't see him. Only then she said I was a liar because *she* didn't see him. He just didn't *want* her to see him. Because she would *hurt* him. Or make somebody *else* hurt him. Grown-ups don't *like* coyotes. They're *scared* of them so they *hurt* them.

Alison wondered how Rachel had figured all of this out. Of course, she had the rich imagination of any seven-year-old, but this was different. It was as if she were repeating something she had heard from someone else. Alison had a thought.

Has the Coyote Lady ever come to your school? she asked.

Rachel eyed her cautiously. When had she lost her daughter's trust? She tried to remember the woman's name, pictured a recent letter to the editor. Natalie Harold. Has Ms. Harold come to your school to talk about the coyotes?

Rachel nodded. Can I go play with my Barbies now? she asked.

As soon as Alison told her yes, Rachel scrambled away. Alison got up and pulled the phone book from the drawer, paged to the H's, and then found the only listing for a Harold in Valle Bosque. Before she lost her nerve, she dialed the number.

In the morning when Rachel waked up she went to the kitchen and there was Molly. Hi Molly, Rachel said, and Molly turned around so fast her coffee jumped out of her cup. God you scared me, Molly said. You must have angel-toes. Rachel liked that, angel-toes, so she made Molly say it again. Then she asked could Molly get down a bowl so she could have some Cheerios and then Molly sat at the table with her and they just talked and talked like grownups while Rachel ate her Cheerios with some banana Molly cut up and put on top and Molly had more coffee and kept looking out the window.

Now brown-hair Barbie makes yellow-hair Barbie sit in Time Out for ten minutes. Yellow-hair Barbie didn't do anything wrong but brown-hair Barbie is the teacher so she is the boss and yellow-hair Barbie has to do what she tells her even though she doesn't like it. She doesn't like brown-hair Barbie either. Brown-hair people are ugly and mean, not like yellow-hair people and not like yellow-hair coyotes, who are Rachel's friends. Yellow-hair Barbie sits in Time Out and talks to her coyote Chris, who is just outside the window because he is her best friend. You are my best friend, says her coyote Chris. You are my best friend, too, says yellow-hair Barbie. Then she leans out the window and kisses him on his nose. His nose is cold and wet. Chris wags his tail. I will be your best friend forever, he says. And I will be your best friend forever too, says yellow-hair Barbie.

three

COYOTE DEBATE AT VILLAGE COUNCIL MEETING

by Tom Sullivan, Beacon *editor*

At the April 7th meeting of the Valle Bosque Village Council, councilors opened discussion on possible methods for keeping coyote-human encounters to a minimum. Villagers were invited to speak, and a number were quite emotional. Kathy Crawford of Entrada de la Salinas tearfully described the carnage left after a coyote entered her rooster pen and destroyed a Rhode Island Red her children were raising as a 4H project

Ms. Crawford reported that there were "feathers everywhere" and talked at length about her children's discovery of the dead rooster. "My kids still cry when they talk about poor Banjo," she said. "I would have shot that coyote in a heartbeat if I'd had my shotgun handy."

Coyote Intelligence founder Natalie Harold spoke as well. "Research has shown that keeping one's chickens in a fully fenced and covered pen will prevent coyote incursions. Ms. Crawford has indicated that her pen was fenced but not covered, and coyotes are high jumpers. We aren't going to change the coyotes. We have to change ourselves."

At this point, Calle la Junta resident Jim Curtis interrupted Ms. Harold from the audience and spoke at length, despite the mayor's efforts to silence him. Much of Mr. Curtis's discourse was met with cheers and applause, especially when he noted that "the best coyote is a dead coyote."

When Mr. Curtis sat down, the mayor encouraged Mrs. Harold to continue, but the coyote activist insisted she had said what she came to say and hoped villagers would keep open minds about the issue.

Because of the late hour, action was tabled until the next meeting.

When Natalie answered the phone, she assumed it was Sherman, calling from his cell to let her know he was making a last stop at the village grocery. Sherman liked to cook, and he was very good at it. Natalie wasn't much of an eater, but it was different eating something she'd watched Sherman cook. She wondered what he was going to make this time and was ready to ask him.

So she was surprised when she heard a woman on the line. Ms. Harold? the woman asked. Her voice was breathy and young.

Yes, Natalie said. I should have checked the Caller ID before I answered, she thought. She didn't want to talk to anyone other than Sherman right now.

Did you speak at the elementary school? the woman continued.

Yes, Natalie said, more comfortable at once. She had spoken to Kay Turner's second grade last week; Kay was part of the informal coyote coalition in the village. This woman was likely another teacher, wanting Natalie to speak to her class, too.

What did you tell them? Now the voice sounded threatening, or frightened, perhaps. Natalie's guard went back up.

Who is this? she asked.

She heard a long inhale and an equally long exhale before the voice continued, more calmly. God, I'm sorry, the woman said. My name's Alison Lomez. My daughter's in Ms. Turner's class, and she said something that made me think you may have spoken to them.

Lomez, Natalie thought. Lomez. Lomez. Then she placed the name: The woman whose daughter had been approached by a coyote while waiting for the school bus. Natalie felt a vein throb in her forehead, the beginning of a headache. What did your daughter say? she asked.

It's not what she said—it's what she thinks *you* said— that kids shouldn't tell adults if they see a coyote because adults will hurt the coyotes.

That is true, said Natalie. She heard the slow, deep

breathing again. She waited for Ms. Lomez to speak without saying anything else.

Ms. Harold, Ms. Lomez began at last, my daughter was approached by a coyote yesterday morning. Now she's named him. After my ex-husband. She says he's her friend. She says she saw him along the *bosque* today. Do you understand, Ms. Harold? Your misinformation could hurt my daughter.

It's highly unlikely a coyote would hurt your daughter, Natalie said. She heard how sanctimonious it sounded.

Well, that's a relief, said Ms. Lomez. Natalie could tell her caller wasn't new to sarcasm.

Ms. Lomez, perhaps you'd like to come over. We could talk. If you come in the early evening, we can sit out on my *portal* and listen to the coyotes sing. I'm not saying you shouldn't be wary of the coyote. But I don't think you need to be frightened.

Alison Lomez laughed, but it was clear she didn't think anything was funny. A coyote threatens my daughter and you're splitting semantic hairs, she said. Tell me: What's the difference between *wary* and *frightened*?

It occurred to Natalie that Ms. Lomez was far brighter than she'd initially assumed, and she berated herself for her prejudice. Will you come over? she persisted. This evening, perhaps?

I'd need to find a sitter. . . More breathing. Natalie found herself breathing in the same rhythm. What time? Ms. Lomez asked at last.

Natalie told her seven o'clock. Just after sunset, she thought. She'd let the coyotes plead their own case.

Sherman arrived shortly after she hung up. As always,

as soon as he came in, Natalie's house felt at once more alive, more connected to the rest of the world. It wasn't that it was no longer her haven; it was because now, for however long he stayed, it was Sherman's haven, too.

Despite the electricity he provided, Sherman looked tired. He looked older. Natalie realized he'd turn fifty this year, but it was the first time he'd really looked his age. It wasn't just the quantity of grey hairs that competed with the black; a deep vertical line had formed a permanent crease between his eyes, as if to separate his forehead in half.

But he was still handsome. It always surprised her, how handsome her brother was. It wasn't something she tended to remember about him, maybe because he was her brother. In public, though, both men and women would turn to look at him. Sherman did his best not to notice, but Natalie knew he did. She knew he didn't like it, either.

As she hung Sherman's coat in the front hall closet, Natalie caught a glimpse of herself in the mirror, and while she saw Sherman's features, there was none of his appeal. Maybe it was the way she wore her own black-and-grey hair, pulled back in a simple ponytail, or her plain black frame glasses. No. Even though she and Sherman resembled each other, she wasn't pretty. It was as if those masculine features couldn't translate to a woman's face. Knowing the burden attractiveness often was to Sherman, Natalie preferred her nondescript anonymity.

In the kitchen, Natalie got out a pitcher and mixed some martinis. She, Sherman, and martinis had a long history. It was how they got caught up. Because it was a relatively mild afternoon, she decided they'd sit out on the *portal*, and she set the pitcher and two martini glasses on a

tray. She opened a jar of olives and dumped its entire contents into a bowl. They weren't just to anchor the martinis:
She and Sherman would eat the others, slowly, one at a
time, just as they had during their parents' long-ago cock-
tail hours.

Natalie called to Sherman that she'd be outside, and he
responded that he'd be right out. The phone rang as the
screen door closed behind her. Let the machine get it, she
thought.

She had just settled into one of the chairs when
Sherman came out, holding the phone toward her. An
Alison Lomez? His eyebrows asked what Natalie could
possibly have to do with someone with a voice like this
woman's.

Natalie sighed and took the phone from him. This is
Natalie, she said.

Ms. Harold? said the breathy voice. I wonder if I could
come by now. My neighbor said she could watch Rachel for
a little while before dinner, but not after. Would that be all
right?

Natalie took her first sip of martini. No, she thought,
that would be not be all right. She felt the all-too-infre-
quent special time she cherished with Sherman slipping
away from her. Say no, she told herself. Say no.

That would be fine, she heard herself say. Then she
clicked off the phone and handed it back to Sherman.
There will be three of us for cocktails, she said. Duty calls.

Coyote duty? Sherman asked. Natalie nodded, then
lifted her glass to the one he'd picked up. Their rims rang
a silver note.

*   *   *

When she saw the silver Lexus with Colorado plates parked in Natalie Harold's driveway, Alison realized she must have company, and felt momentarily sorry to intrude. Then she decided she had no reason to feel sorry about anything. She meant to tell Ms. Harold what it felt like to watch a coyote sit down next to your seven-year-old daughter. She meant to tell her what it felt like to have your husband, your high school sweetheart for God's sake, up and leave you for a younger woman. She meant to tell her what it felt like to have everything you ever believed in pulled out from under you, how it felt to find out that under that illusory rug there was no foundation whatsoever.

Get a grip, she told herself as she locked her minivan. The only thing she was here to talk about was the coyote. She wanted to find out if there was something she could do to make it leave Rachel alone. And she wanted to find out if she was right to feel as threatened by the coyote as she did. Ms. Harold might prefer coyotes to people (or so her letter-writing antagonists claimed), but no one in the village knew more about the animals than she did.

Alison's knock on the door was answered by a man so movie star handsome that Alison was rendered speechless. Richard Gere, she thought, momentarily confused. What was Richard Gere doing at Natalie Harold's house? Then he said, You must be Ms. Lomez. Come in. I'm Natalie's brother, Sherman. Sherman Gold. He offered his hand. Alison shook it. The phrase *get a grip* took on added meaning.

Alison, she said, Alison Lomez, hoping she wasn't blushing. She realized she *was* staring, and looked away.

Come in, Alison, Sherman Gold said. He smiled. Alison smiled back. She wished she'd brushed her hair, then caught a glimpse of herself in the hall mirror as they passed it and saw the serviceable haircut and highlighting she'd gotten a few weeks before were doing their job. Her green eyes looked tired, though. She touched her hair quickly and moved on before Sherman noticed.

He led her through the old adobe house's cluttered living room—the furniture looked as if it might have been expensive thirty years before—into the kitchen and then out onto the east-facing *portal*. Natalie Harold was curled in an old wicker chair, sipping a martini. She looked familiar, but Alison didn't think they'd met before. Ms. Harold held out her hand and Alison shook it. Something about Ms. Harold made Alison feel as if she'd been allowed an audience with the Queen. Please sit down, Ms. Harold said. Would you like a martini? They're a family tradition. Sherman only just arrived.

Oh, I'm so sorry, Alison said. I didn't know—

Ms. Harold waved her protest away and pointed to the martini pitcher. Alison had never had a martini. All right, she said. Ms. Harold dropped an olive into a glass, stirred the contents of the pitcher once, then poured through a shaker. She handed the glass to Alison.

Sit, she said. Alison sat. Sherman sat, too. Alison was struck by the juxtaposition of physical weakness and charismatic authority that Natalie Harold projected. It occurred to Alison that with contact lenses and a good haircut, she would be a striking woman.

What is it I can tell you? Ms. Harold asked.

Alison looked at Sherman. He gave her an encouraging smile. No wedding ring, she noticed. God, he was stunning. What must it be like to be so gorgeous? Alison thought it must be awful. Then she realized why Ms. Harold looked familiar—they looked alike.

Ms. Lomez?

Alison laughed her fake laugh, the short exhale through her nose accompanied by a tight-lipped grin that she suspected didn't fool anyone. I can't tell you the last time I relaxed, she said. She raised her glass and took sip of the martini. The taste was a paradox—a dryness that it didn't seem something wet could have, a bitterness that was pleasant. She took another sip and then set her glass down.

My husband left me, she said. No, no, no—that was not how she meant to begin. I'm a single parent, she tried. Good. That was better. It's hard. I work full-time, and then I try to be there for Rachel, too. Sometimes being there for Rachel suffers.

Natalie Harold and Sherman Gold watched her without responding, each with the same encouragement in their eyes. Alison wondered if they were twins.

Alison lifted her glass and took another sip of martini. I don't know what to think about the coyote, she said. I called Animal Control and the man said—

Ms. Harold interrupted her. Ralph Sandoval or Frank Sebold?

Ralph Sandoval. Ms. Harold nodded and Alison continued. He said he didn't think a coyote would hurt a child. But he wasn't sure. And how I felt—I'm not sure I can even tell you how I felt. She paused and looked toward the mountain, swallowed hard and then continued. Like I'd forgotten how to swallow, she said. Like I'd never known how to breathe. She stopped and took a deep breath and then went on. Like someone had ripped my heart out. She paused again, and in the pause found the words that described the feeling precisely. Like they'd set something hard, something *foreign* in its place.

She felt the way Sherman Gold was looking at her change as she said this. He'd been listening attentively, she'd been sure of that, but now he seemed to be looking at her with an added interest. You *wish*, she thought.

Anyway, I thought I'd ask you. If a coyote would hurt a child. If *that* coyote would hurt *my* child. If there's something I can do to make it stop.

Before Ms. Harold could respond, the sound of a jet intruded. As if on cue, a coyote yipped, and then another, in a different voice. Ms. Harold tilted her head to one side and smiled at her brother, who tilted his head in precisely the same way and smiled the same way, too, lips closed.

More coyote voices joined in. These sounded younger, as if they were pups, maybe. Alison tried to count how many different voices there were. Then some dogs—next door, it sounded like—started barking, confusing the music into a cacophony. The coyote chorus ceased as quickly as it had begun.

Natalie Harold looked at Alison as if she were waiting for her to say something. Alison tried to remember what she'd just said, but couldn't. They sound so, so *wild*, she said.

Yes, said Ms. Harold. She was still smiling.

But like a family, Alison said.

Yes.

Alison felt something click into place in her mind. You wanted me to hear them, she said. So I'd understand that they're a family.

Yes.

Alison thought about it. She thought about her own fractured family, about Chris's deceptive veneer of protection, her own cautious daily dance along the thin rope of her new life without him. At least animals knew their boundaries, she thought. Or usually did. She remembered something she'd read recently in the *Albuquerque Journal*. But look what's happened with the wolf reintroduction down in the Gila, she said.

You mean that some have disappeared? Ms. Harold said. She wasn't smiling anymore.

Alison looked at Sherman Gold. He wasn't smiling anymore, either. Alison set her drink down. That they've killed sheep. Adult sheep.

Natalie Harold suddenly reached across the small wicker table that divided them and put her hand on Alison's arm. Ms. Lomez, she said.

Alison.

Alison. I promise you the coyote will not hurt your daughter. Natalie Harold's eyes held hers in a steady, calm gaze. I promise.

Alison thought of Chris. Of how promises could be broken. But she wanted to believe Natalie Harold. All right, she said. All right.

Sherman came back outside after he'd seen Alison Lomez to the front door. He settled into his chair before he spoke.

I hope you're not sorry you made that promise, he said.

Natalie couldn't think how to respond to him, not right away. She'd had to promise the woman the coyote wouldn't hurt her daughter. She was sure it wouldn't. But—and this is what Sherman knew—she wasn't positive.

Is there something she can do? Sherman went on. Can she make herself big? He raised his arms over his head in pantomime. Could the coyote be relocated?

Natalie finished off her first martini and stirred the contents of the pitcher before pouring another through the shaker. She topped off Sherman's glass, too, and then they clinked rims.

You like her, she said.

Sherman smiled, looked off toward the mountain, which was donning its all-too-brief pink cloak. *Sandia*, the mountain's name, was the Spanish word for watermelon.

She's young, Sherman.

Natalie could tell he'd decided not to listen. She hoped that whatever happened between him and Alison Lomez wouldn't hurt Alison Lomez too much in the end.

To the editor:

Yesterday morning, as I was driving to work, I saw the most incredible thing: A coyote was walking along the side of the road, as if this were its everyday routine.

When I got closer, I saw that it was carrying something, but it wasn't until I'd drawn parallel that I realized that it was a black cat. The cat was dead, of course. But what struck me most—and I have a black cat of my own—was how natural it seemed. It was like stopping at Starbucks on your way to work. I laughed when I thought that, laughed at myself for anthropomorphizing the coyote, and laughed at how awful it was that I'd thought it. It could have been my Howard the coyote had just killed. I had a momentary flash of fear, in fact, until I remembered that Howard had been sleeping in his chair in the bedroom when I left.

The thing is, once I knew it wasn't Howard, I thought it was fine. It was someone else's cat. And then I thought how interesting it was that as long as it was someone else's cat, I didn't care. I couldn't help it. I thought of how I felt about Iraq, about Afghanistan and the Middle East and wherever it is in Africa they're dying this week. I even thought of 9-11, and I didn't think, There but for the grace of God, go I. *I* thought, As long as it doesn't touch me, it can't hurt me.

I don't know why I'm being so forthcoming in a letter to the editor, but it struck me somehow, all of it. I realized that if I don't give a damn, who will? I consider myself well-informed, and not just because of what I do. I read the papers, I vote, I volunteer, I contribute to charities. But every night, I come home to my acre in Valle Bosque—we all come home to our acres in Valle Bosque, don't we?—and close my door to the horrors of the larger world.

That's when I realized I can't just close my door anymore. I've got to begin somewhere. And so I'm going to begin here, at home, with that coyote carrying someone's dead cat down the road. I think Natalie Harold is wrong. I think the coyotes are very different from us, and that all our care and understanding won't change the fact that they will kill us—and those we care about—if we let them.

Thanks for providing this forum for local voices. I know I'm not the only Valle Bosqueleño who appreciates it.

Sincerely,

Sharon Putnam

Editor's Note: Dr. Putnam teaches history at the University of New Mexico.

When she got back from Natalie Harold's, Alison started dinner. Rachel brought two Barbies, one blonde and one brunette, into the kitchen, where they interacted in whispers. It wasn't until Alison noticed what the Barbies were wearing that she realized Rachel was still wearing the outfit she'd put together herself that morning.

Rachel had been unusually quiet after Alison picked her up. Alison thought it must be because of the *bosque* field trip she'd taken with her class that day. But by the time she got dinner on the table—macaroni and cheese, simple and one of Rachel's favorites—Rachel's eyes were half-closed. Are you sleepy, Swee'pea? Alison asked her, and Rachel, who usually fought any suggestion that she was tired, nodded slowly. How about you take your bath right after dinner and then we can snuggle up and read?

Okay, Rachel said. She steered an oranged elbow of macaroni around her plate. On the table next to it, the Barbies lay abandoned, arms and legs akimbo.

Alison decided there was no sense forcing dinner conversation and soon found herself thinking of Sherman Gold. She was certain something had changed in the way he looked at her when she'd said how she felt when the coyote threatened Rachel. She tried to remember her exact words. Something about how she'd forgotten how to swallow? Or how to breathe? Like someone had—what was it?—torn her heart out and—yes, this was it—put something hard there instead.

No, that wasn't it, not exactly. Besides, she wasn't sure if it were what she'd said or how she'd said it that had made Sherman Gold look at her in that new way. If it were *what* she'd said, it meant he was attracted by her love for her daughter. But if it were *how* she'd said it, it was the way she phrased things.

A lot of people teased her about the way she phrased things—a walking dictionary, Chris used to call her, and not always kindly, either—so Alison sometimes worked at what she thought of as talking down. Especially in the construction business, this seemed a good idea, to not sound too smart, or, at any rate, too well-educated.

It wasn't as if Alison had been born to it, not the way Natalie Harold and Sherman Gold seemed to have been. Alison believed that people who'd been born rich didn't think too much about the way they talked—or about anything else, for that matter. People who'd been born rich drank martinis on their *portals* at 5 p.m., while people like Alison were making their small children macaroni and cheese. No wonder people who'd been born rich didn't have anything to do with those who hadn't. Of course, she told herself, if they got to know each other individually, well, then, that would be different.

Opposites attract, she thought. Then she smiled. Last night, she'd been convinced a man would never notice her again. Tonight, not only had a man noticed her, he'd been a man unlike any who'd ever noticed her before.

A movement alerted Alison to her surroundings: Rachel's head nodding slowly toward sleep. Alison reached to move the bowl of macaroni and cheese out of the way, then watched as her daughter's head dropped slowly to the table. After a moment of gazing fondly and absently at the sleeping child, Alison got up and carried Rachel to her room.

The trees don't have leaves, but they have scary black arms, and the arms try to catch Rachel but she runs and runs and runs. Teacher isn't there anymore and no one else is either. It is just Rachel, running through the scary trees and it makes her tired so she lies down and goes to sleep. Then Chris her coyote is there, kissing her and telling her a story. Rachel doesn't tell him he can't really talk because he is talking, isn't he, so she listens to the story he is telling her about how Molly is really her Mommy. That is why Molly French-braided Rachel's hair so good and lets Rachel wear the clothes she wants. But now Rachel looks down and sees that she's not wearing any clothes at all! Mommy will be very mad because those clothes were very expensive and doesn't Rachel know they don't have any money since Daddy went to live with Didi? Rachel starts crying because she doesn't have her clothes and then Chris says—he is up in the tree now and the tree is not so scary—well I don't have any clothes, either, so why don't you just live with me in my tree? But when Rachel tries to climb up, she can't, because the arms of the tree are holding her down and she gets scared and can't move. She tries and tries and gets more and more scared and then she cries and calls for Mommy and then she wakes up and Mommy is there.

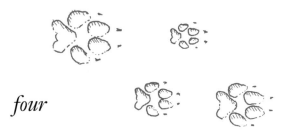

four

In some respects . . . a man is a good deal like a coyote.

Sherman was already up when Natalie came into the kitchen at seven. I made coffee, he said. Do you still take cream?

Natalie nodded and sat down at the table. She wasn't a morning person, not like Sherman was. When they were children, he'd handled mornings for both of them. She didn't really awaken till they'd gone down the elevator, past the doorman, and out the door. Even though he was younger, it was he who had walked her to her school, and then continued on alone to his. Both private schools, of course. It was what one did, in Manhattan.

Natalie pictured that trajectory as she sat looking out

her window at the ready-to-bud trees bending in the April wind. Another week and they'd be green, she thought. She loved how you could chart time without a calendar when you lived amongst natural things. Spring here meant winds so angry they scoured the earth clean. The greening of what little greened in a desert followed, as if it required that cleansing before it could occur.

Spring meant wild babies, too, not just the coyotes, but the swallows who returned to her *portal* each year. They were the same swallows, she was certain of it. They'd examine the nest they'd abandoned the previous fall, then swoop in with dried grasses to repair any damage (though the tidy mud bowls they tucked into the eaves were remarkably strong), and then settle in until the hatchlings arrived. When they did, mama and papa bird would take turns shuttling back and forth to fill the tiny beaks Natalie could just barely see over the edge of the nest.

The sun topped Sandia mountain, and Natalie squinted toward it while she sipped her coffee. Across from her, Sherman was flipping pages of the Albuquerque *Journal*, perhaps seeking some tidbit of real news among the ads for bras and cellular phones and miracle anti-wrinkle creams. On Sunday mornings, Natalie would pick up the *New York Times* at the small local market. No other paper seemed worth reading when you'd been brought up with the *Times*.

Natalie finished her coffee and stood to make toast. Sherman looked up. I cut up some melon, he said. Mixed in some berries. It's in the fridge.

Bless you, said Natalie. Sherman spoiled her. No, that wasn't what Sherman did at all. Sherman did not operate with a motive, not when it came to her, at any rate. He simply did what he did. It was why they were so comfortable with each other.

Natalie was dishing some fruit into a bowl when the phone rang. It was Ralph Sandoval, which surprised her. It was early for anyone to call. And while Ralph never called at all, now he had called her two mornings in a row.

Ms. Harold? That trap I set yesterday? Someone called. We got us a coyote.

After Rachel's nightmare, Alison had carried her daughter in to sleep with her, and now Rachel was up early. That was the problem with letting her fall asleep before her regular bedtime, Alison thought, rolling over with a groan. Alison herself had been up late, staring at the wall next to the bed, thinking about Sherman Gold. She knew she shouldn't, but her mind seemed to have—ha!—a mind of its own. She pictured the color of his eyes, a green speckled with gold, and his hair, also two-toned, as if one shade weren't enough to color someone like him. She thought about the casual way the sleeves of his white cotton shirt were rolled, to just below the elbows, of the way he wore his jeans, beltless. He'd been barefoot, and she thought about the kind of person who could pull that off. A studied casualness, she thought, then was certain she'd read the term somewhere else and felt unaccountably guilty.

Now she lay in bed thinking the same things all over again, while on the pillow beside her the two Barbies engaged in a pitched battle that involved shrieking on both their parts. When Alison couldn't stand it anymore, she opened one eye to see if she could ascertain the cause of the fight.

You need to go to bed, insisted the darker-haired of the two dolls. For emphasis, she entangled her pointed plastic hand in the blonde doll's silky hair.

No! shrieked the blonde Barbie. You can't make me! Then she was on her back, the better for the other Barbie to drag her under the covers and tuck her in.

Sleep-tight-don't-let-the-bedbugs-bite, said the darker-haired Barbie. That was when Rachel must have felt Alison watching her. The dark-haired Barbie planted a kiss on the blonde Barbie's forehead, and Rachel turned and smiled. Hi, Mommy, she said. Is it time to get up yet?

Alison looked out toward the mountain for an answer and saw that the sun hadn't yet cleared Sandia Peak. That meant it was still before seven. Still, if she got up now, they could have a leisurely breakfast, without any of the hurrying weekday mornings usually demanded. You bet it is, Alison said. How about we make pancake people? Usually reserved for weekends, pancake people were a favorite of Rachel's.

Yay! Rachel cried, clapping her hands. She slid off the bed, leaving one Barbie to sleep and the other where she'd been abandoned.

While she mixed batter, Alison looked east toward the sunrise. That was the direction Natalie Harold's house was, too, in the irrigated older section of the village that sloped gently down to the Rio Grande. Alison wondered if Sherman Gold was up yet, if he too were watching the way the sun topped the mountain. Alison pictured him in the kitchen they'd passed through on their way to the *portal*, hands in the pockets of his jeans, watching the sun rise, just as she was. Maybe he was thinking the same thing, she thought, wondering if she too were watching the sunrise.

Rachel had pulled a chair over to the stove and now stood on it with crossed arms, waiting for Alison to pour the batter into the pan. Rachel had collected her pancake people accessories and scattered them on the counter next to the stove: a squeeze bottle of butter for the eyes, nose, and hair and a jar of grape jelly and a jelly spoon to design the mouth. Focusing on the task at hand with effort, Alison poured the batter into a rough oval, then added a few drops above for hair. Rachel giggled, then settled down to wait.

Alison poured herself a cup of coffee and Rachel a glass of milk, set them on the table, and returned to the stove to flip the now-whole pancake person. Can I do his face now? Rachel asked, and Alison nodded. Then she watched as her daughter turned what had been at least passably human into the remarkably accurate likeness of a smiling coyote.

To the editor:

Thank you for printing Dr. Putnam's letter. I can understand her concern. I am certain it was horrifying to see someone's dead pet in the mouth of a coyote. But this is precisely why we should not let our cats wander out-of-doors. Dr. Putnam has unfortunately drawn the wrong conclusion from her experience. Would she choose to destroy the swallow because it catches the fly? The rabbit because it nibbles the grasses? Killing the coyote because it stalks its prey is no different from killing the trout because it swallows the minnow. This is not about war and enemies. It's about peaceful coexistence, and learning to respect the ways of one's neighbors, no matter how different they might be.

As always, thank you for the valuable forum this letters column provides.

Sincerely,

Natalie Harold

To the editor:

That Harold woman is wrong as usual. If coyotes had any idea of how to "peacefully coexist," well, then, that would be different. But all they want is what's ours— our land, our animals, our livelihoods. Coyotes are killers, plain and simple. They're not thinking about changing their ways to accommodate us. Why should we change our ways to accommodate them? Hasn't that Natalie Harold ever heard of survival of the fittest? I say, may the best man win.

Jim Curtis

Ralph Sandoval picked Natalie up in front of her house a little before eight. She'd asked Sherman to come along, but he hadn't wanted to. I'll do the dishes and straighten up the house, he said. Coyotes are your thing. He didn't add what they both knew, that women were his. Women were what saw Sherman through every crisis, although they didn't often realize this was their role. Natalie knew Sherman had already selected Alison Lomez to see him through this one. He was probably going to figure out a way to run into her. He might even call her. Natalie didn't tell him not to. She didn't bring it up at all.

In the end, the women Sherman romanced were all-too-soon surprised by the sudden change in him once he'd gotten himself back together again. Like Humpty Dumpty, Sherman climbed—and fell from—a lot of walls. But unlike Mother Goose's unhappy egg, Sherman put himself back together so well that only Natalie could see the cracks. The long string of women who facilitated the repair saw only the lovely and seemingly intact shell and not the complicated person inside.

Ralph was unusually talkative this morning, so Natalie couldn't dwell on Sherman and his ways for long. Ralph was driving the truck she hated, outfitted with four doors on each side which opened to small compartments to hold captured animals. Sometimes when that truck drove by, Natalie was certain she could smell the fear those compartments had housed, a sour and unhappy smell that said as much about the captor as it did the captive.

Ralph was talking about Nina's hamburger, how she'd said it would be just the bait, and how she'd been right. Natalie loved to hear Ralph talk about Nina. Another man might feel obligated to insert a degree of sarcasm or long-suffering, but Ralph and Nina shared a mutual respect rare not just among spouses but particularly, it seemed, among those who had lived together for a long time. Nina was a district librarian down in Albuquerque, and she and Natalie had at one time belonged to the same book group.

The group had broken up after one of its members, a dynamic woman in her 80s, died. Natalie missed the camaraderie, and it occurred to her that she should call Nina to see if they could somehow resurrect it.

Usually I make the hamburger, Ralph was saying, but Nina said my hamburger would probably run off not just the coyote but the snakes and fire ants, too. I use green chiles is why. Right in the meat.

By now they were traveling the same stretch of ditch road they'd driven the day before. Ralph pulled up just shy of the adobe yard and shut off the truck. Its engine ticked a rhythm that slowed and then stopped. Natalie became aware of another sound, a scritch-scritch-scritch coming from where she knew the trap was. She could feel the hair on the back of her neck prickle, while at the same time she felt a sudden solid lump inside that she inexplicably remembered Alison Lomez describing the night before. That was when she realized that what she was feeling might well be fear.

She wasn't afraid of the coyote, that wasn't it. She was afraid of how the coyote would be. She tried to imagine the reaction of an animal—of anyone—who'd always been free, suddenly trapped in a small enclosure. Would it be like the way Sherman got when one of the women started talking about moving in with him, or worse, getting married? Sherman would turn sullen and then mean, snapping at the woman as though his words could destroy her. Startled by the change, the woman would wonder what had caused it, but then, because of the kind of woman to whom Sherman was attracted, she wouldn't stick around. Fuck this, the last one, Sheila, had said. Fuck this and fuck you.

Natalie remembered how Sherman had laughed as he'd told her this, but she knew he was laughing because by then he'd already escaped.

Ralph had slid from the truck and was walking slowly and deliberately toward the half-buried cage. The scratching sound hadn't altered, which meant the coyote hadn't noticed Ralph's approach, and Natalie took advantage of its ignorance to climb down from the cab and drop in behind Ralph. She noticed that not only were her hands shaking, her palms were damp despite the cool morning. But really, now: Could what they'd find in the cage possibly be worse than what she'd already imagined?

The cage was still hidden in the dried grass where Ralph had buried it. Wearing heavy gloves, Ralph brushed away the debris until the top of the cage was exposed. The scratching stopped. Natalie waited for the snap of jaws, the low growl, but that was not what the coyote did. Instead, it sat down on its haunches and looked at them with eyes of a yellow it didn't seem possible eyes could be, first at Ralph and then at Natalie. What took you so long? it seemed to be asking. That was when Natalie realized that she was crying, and had been for some time.

Today in school there is something wrong with Rachel's tummy. First she has to go to the bathroom and then she has to go to the bathroom again and teacher gets mad but she lets her go. When she has to go to the bathroom again, teacher comes out in the hall with her and asks her why does she have to keep going to the bathroom. That makes Rachel cry, so then teacher puts her hand on Rachel's forehead like

Mommy does and then she says, Oh dear, and tells Rachel to go see the nurse right away.

Rachel has never gone to see the nurse before but she knows where he is because teacher showed everyone the first day of school. The nurse's room has a smell Rachel doesn't like and there is a bigger boy in there with him that she doesn't like either who is sitting on a table. Rachel stands by the door watching them with her tummy hurting and she wants to go to the bathroom again but she doesn't move because she's scared. She might be scared of the boy or she might be scared of the nurse or she might be scared of something she doesn't even know what, but her scared-edness makes her stand there and not say anything forever and ever. Then the boy looks at her and makes a mean face that the nurse sees so the nurse turns around. Well, hello, he says. What can I do for you?

Rachel doesn't want to answer him because she doesn't want the big boy to know what's the matter. But then her tummy hurts her more again so she tells him, My tummy hurts. Teacher told me to come and see you.

What's your name?

Rachel Lomez.

And who's your teacher, Rachel Lomez?

Ms. Turner. I am in the second grade.

Hop down, he says to the big boy. There's nothing wrong with you a swift kick in the pants wouldn't cure. The big boy jumps off the table like a cat and then waits while the nurse writes on a pad and then tears the piece of paper off and hands it to him. Back to class, the nurse says. And don't come knocking unless you're at death's door.

When the big boy walks by he bumps into Rachel.

You're at death's door, he says, real low so the nurse can't hear. Then he laughs and goes away.

Oh, dear, says the nurse. Pay no attention to Richard. Rachel watches the nurse pull the paper on the table like a roll of toilet paper and then he tears off a piece and puts it in a metal can he opens with his foot. It closes again when his foot lets go. Rachel wants to go see this can but she stays by the door.

Come in, Rachel Lomez, the nurse says. Can you climb up on this table? Attagirl. Now, what seems to be the trouble? Your tummy? Oh my. Well. Let's take your temperature, shall we?

After the nurse takes Rachel's temperature, he tells her to sit tight, so she tries to sit as tight as she can while in the next room she hears him on the phone asking someone for Mommy's phone number at work.

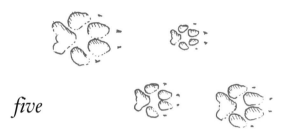

five

Neither bark nor howl of [a trapped] animal has the sound of one that is free.

It's probably just a twenty-four-hour bug, the nurse told Alison. It's been going around. Still, all the way home, Alison snuck glimpses of Rachel in the rearview mirror, noting her flushed face and the line of sweat where her hair met her forehead.

Rachel had been sick before. Like all kids her age, she brought home a malady per month, colds and fevers and less-defined sneezes and sniffles. This was no different than the others, yet Alison felt herself full of an unaccountable fear.

Once in the house, she settled Rachel into bed and then returned with a glass of ginger ale, which she dispensed from a tablespoon according to the nurse's instructions. Two children's Tylenol followed, and then a swallow of Pepto Bismol. Rachel grimaced at the last. Good.

Can I bring you anything else? Alison asked, brushing the damp hair off her daughter's warm forehead. Rachel shook her head. You want to sleep some, Swee'pea? Logy, Rachel nodded. Okay, then. I'll be just down the hall. Rachel's eyes had already closed.

Being home on a weekday morning always felt illicit, much the way playing hooky or sneaking into a bar underage once had, and Alison wandered through the house, plumping pillows and straightening pictures. In the living room, she stood for a time in the center of the room, looking out toward the now-bright mountain. How much it changed from moment to moment, she thought. She could stand here all day watching and it would never appear the same twice.

When the phone rang, Alison was first startled then worried. What if the nurse had learned something dangerous was making the rounds of Valle Bosque Elementary? She raced to the kitchen to answer before the phone woke Rachel, so her hello was even more breathless than usual.

Alison? The male voice was familiar, but it wasn't the school nurse and it wasn't anyone from work. Who would call her here, during the day? Alison responded cautiously.

It's Sherman Gold, the voice said. I met you last night at my sister Natalie Harold's. I wasn't sure I'd find you home.

Alison felt her breath catch and her heartbeat quicken. She sank into one of the kitchen chairs and inhaled deeply before she spoke. My daughter's home sick, she said.

Oh—is it—?

Kids bring home a bug a week, it seems like, Alison interrupted breezily, as if she hadn't been sick with fear herself a moment before. As if she weren't breathless with the knowledge that he had called her. Sherman Gold had called her. He was talking to her now.

So you get to play hooky, Sherman said. Alison was struck by the echo of her own thought, then decided to complete it.

It's like sneaking into a bar underage, she said.

Sherman laughed. You know, when Nat and I were growing up, the drinking age in New York was eighteen. The joke was if you wanted to get your finger on the pulse of New York high schoolers, you need look no further than your corner pub.

Alison laughed her fake laugh and tried to think of something to say. I didn't know that, she said at last. Oh, Alison, she thought. You can do better.

Where are *you* from? Sherman asked her.

Alison forced herself to relax. Here, she said. Well, sort of. I grew up in Albuquerque. In the Valley.

A native, Sherman said. Not many of those around.

For some reason, Alison thought of the coyote. Chris. The coyote Rachel called Chris. My husband—my ex-husband—and I are both natives, she said. God, Alison, what a stupid thing to say.

Do you mind talking to an interloper like me? Sherman asked.

This time Alison laughed her real laugh. That depends, she said. On why you're calling.

Something you said last night made me think of a

poem I read, he said. Did that ever happen to you, where you get this *frisson* of recognition that you can't place? Drives me crazy.

Yes, Alison said. *Frisson*, she thought. She liked the way Sherman Gold phrased things, the way she imagined she herself would if she lived in a world like his.

Anyway, Nat's got all of our mother's old poetry books—she was a writer, Mother—as well as quite a few of her own, so last night I paged through some of them. I actually expected to find it, and maybe that's why I did. So—don't laugh—I just wanted to read it to you. Is that okay?

While Sherman spoke, Alison felt a growing contentment, as if her own mother had discovered her shivering and carefully covered her with a blanket. Oh, she said. That would be lovely. It was not a way she ordinarily spoke, *That would be lovely*, but it was, at this moment, precisely how she felt.

Without preamble, Sherman read.

> *There's a soft spot in everything*
> *Our fingers touch,*
>   *the one place where everything breaks*
> *When we press it just right.*
> *The past is like that with its arduous edges and blind*
>   *sides,*
> *The whorls of our fingerprints*
>   *embedded along its walls*
> *Like fossils the sea has left behind.*

Read it again, Alison said.

It's by Charles Wright, said Sherman. From a poem called *Two Stories*.

Read it again, Alison commanded.

He read. There's a lot more, he said when he stopped this time. I can read the whole poem.

No, Alison said. She was thinking about *the one place where everything breaks/when we press it just right*. She was thinking how broken she felt herself. She was thinking how remarkable it was that Sherman Gold, a man she'd met briefly and peripherally the night before, had found the words to express the way she'd been feeling ever since the day Chris left. Please don't, she said; any more would press too hard.

I knew it was the right poem, he said.

I'd like to see it, she said. Then she told him where she lived.

Natalie had always cautioned herself not to humanize the coyote, but face to face, it was difficult not to. What else but reason would impel a caged animal to meet the eyes of its captor? What else but educated intelligence would keep it from panic in an unfamiliar situation?

Hey, Pup, Ralph Sandoval was saying. You're a smart fella, aren't you?

Male? Natalie asked, as much to ground herself as for the answer.

I'd say only a few years old, from the looks of him. Good hamburger, huh, guy? Ralph pressed in toward the cage and lowered his voice. You'd like mine even better.

Natalie wondered if Ralph were lightening the moment

just for her. She brushed her cheek with the back of her hand, then smiled at him only because she did not laugh easily. What now? she asked.

I should have brought the other truck, Ralph said. Frank had it out when I left and I didn't want to wait. But I can't transfer our friend from the cage to a hold on my own, even if I could get the loop around his neck, which I doubt. Frank should be back by now, though. Only thing is, he'd have my hide if he knew you were with me.

I could sit here with him while you swapped trucks, Natalie said. It wouldn't take you more than five, ten minutes.

Ralph looked from the caged coyote to Natalie. You don't mind?

She smiled again. The only thing I'd like better would be if he would sit here with me without the cage to hold him.

Ralph studied the caged coyote a moment more. You won't tell Frank? he said at last.

No one will ever know, said Natalie. There are moments that aren't meant to be shared. This is one of them.

I'll be right back, Ralph said. And then Natalie and the coyote were alone.

Maybe, Alison thought, it was because she was alone. The usual warning signs didn't seem to apply. *Beware of men bearing poetry*, Molly would have said, or, *For a smart woman, you sure can be dumb*, so Alison willed her brand of wisdom away. Like other books of its ilk, *Own Your Own Life* cautioned that spurned women were easy prey for what the author called hit-and-run men, but instinct told Alison that Sherman Gold was different. She had to learn to trust men again. She had to learn to trust *herself* again. Why not start here? Why not start now?

Alison tiptoed to the doorway of Rachel's bedroom and looked in at her sleeping daughter. Light fluted snores punctuated Rachel's breathing. Alison smiled. *There's a soft spot in everything*, Sherman had read. And those are the places we try hardest to keep covered, Alison thought. She stepped into the room to adjust the blanket where it had slipped from Rachel's shoulder.

Alison was in the kitchen making a fresh pot of coffee when she heard the light tap on the door. How thoughtful of him to not ring the bell, she thought as she walked to foyer and then opened the door to him. Come in, she said with a sweep of her arm. I'm making coffee.

Sherman held up a white paper bag. And I brought muffins, he said. Carrot-raisin. Is that okay?

That's perfect, Alison said, even though she'd never tried a carrot-raisin muffin before. It *would* be perfect. It would be her Proustian madeleine, she was sure of it. She led him into the kitchen, where he stood looking out the window while she busied herself with cups and plates.

Look where he's standing, Alison noted. It was where she had stood that morning, thinking about him. She thought about that now, wondering if what she'd thought remained in the place she'd thought it, would now some-how communicate itself to Sherman, forge a connection between them.

There was already a connection between them. She

could feel it even with his back to her, the thread of it, silken and invisible and powerful. She tugged. He turned and looked at her.

Do you take cream? she asked easily and he nodded. She poured the same amount into each cup and then carried them to the table. While she got out placemats and napkins, Sherman retrieved the plates she'd taken down and placed a muffin on each.

A royal banquet, he said when they'd both sat down, then lifted his coffee cup in mock toast. Mm, he said after a sip.

Alison broke off a corner from the top of the muffin and tasted it. It was good—not sweet, like supermarket muffins. Where'd you get these? she asked. She was surprised when Sherman blushed.

I made them, he said. I always do that, when I get to Nat's, go through her larder for fading fruits and veggies and then whip them into a muffin stew. This time it was stale raisins and latter-day carrots. Anything old is new again in a muffin.

Alison had begun to smile at the phrase *latter-day carrots*, which had made her think of Molly, and his solemn pronouncement that *anything old is new again in a muffin* made her laugh. The Gospel of muffins, she said when she stopped laughing.

Why not? Sherman said. He was struggling not to smile, she could tell. Why not base our Gospels on the everyday?

God's in the details, Alison said.

The miraculous is in the mundane, said Sherman.

Alison smiled. That's what I said.

So you did. Then he did smile. He finished his coffee, and rose before she could move. No—I'll get it. Enjoy your muffin. After retrieving the pot, he poured himself more coffee and topped hers off, then sat down again. How's your daughter? he asked.

Rachel, she said. She'll be fine. She's already fine—she's sleeping it off, whatever *it* was. It might have been the pancake people we made for breakfast. But she hardly ate last night, so it must have started sooner—

Pancake people?

Alison smiled. I let her decorate her pancakes with faces. She thought about the coyote that had materialized in this morning's pancake and felt her smile fade, but decided not to mention it. I don't think it was breakfast. It's a bug. Kids get them all the time. Moms get some R&R. Fair trade all around.

Except for the sick kid.

Kids don't feel illness the same way we do. They hurt, sure, but there's none of the associated fear of it being something more serious or guilt over missing work. There have even been some studies that suggest they may not feel pain as acutely.

Oh, to be a child again, Sherman said, and not feel pain acutely.

Alison thought of Chris. Go away, she commanded, and he vanished. Who's to say we can't be children? she said to Sherman. Just for a day. I'm already playing hooky. What about you?

I'm between jobs, he said, crumbling the last bit of muffin onto his plate. As they watched the crumbs settle haphazardly, Alison felt the first stitch of awkwardness.

What do you do? she asked to pull it tight again.

Sherman smiled and brushed the crumbs from his fingers. Well, that depends, he said. Most recently, I was the CEO of an Internet start-up.

Uh-oh, Alison said.

Sherman nodded. Exactly, he said. Before that, I was in real estate. Both in Denver.

Alison mentally calculated how, now that the speed limit on the interstate had been raised to 75, Denver was much closer than it once had been.

What do *you* do? he asked her.

I handle PR for High Mesa Construction. I'm on their big interstate job right now. Maybe you've heard about it.

He nodded. PR. You fix things with words.

That's not really what PR is, Alison said. My job is to paint an accurate and positive picture.

Aren't they mutually exclusive?

Not always. Not often. No. Not ever. Alison warmed into her standard defense of public relations speech. People think PR is about spin, about managing information, and, it's true, those are aspects of it. But the gist of it is just what it's called: public relations. Helping the public understand what we're doing. Good PR is the same as good communication: It's clear, it's concise, and it's— Alison stopped. She was going to say *honest*, but for some reason didn't.

Sherman held his hand out in mock defeat. All right, all right, he said. I'm convinced. Hell, I'm a convert. You got a bridge you want to sell me, too?

Alison blushed, reached for her coffee cup to cover her embarrassment, then realized it was empty and set it down again. Why was she embarrassed? She was proud of what she did for a living, and she was damned good at it, besides. Look at yesterday, how she'd averted a PR disaster. She thought about telling Sherman Gold about that, as an example, but something stopped her. Was it because someone had died? Well, he had died through his own negligence. Spin the spinner, Alison thought. Weave the web.

Hello? Sherman said, leaning toward her. Anybody in there? Alison smiled. I lost you there for a minute, he said. Deep thoughts?

You were going to show me the poem, Alison said. But you know what? If we're going to play hooky, deep thoughts can't be allowed.

You're right, Sherman said. If we're going to break the rules, we'd better do it in style. Like Calvinball. You remember Calvinball?

Calvin and Hobbes, Alison said. I don't even read the funnies anymore, now that they're gone.

So the only rule is that there are no rules. Just for the day. Deal? He held out his hand.

Alison reached across the table and shook it. His hand was warm and his handshake strong. Alison didn't want to let go, but she did, quickly. Deal, she said. So the hell with clearing this table. Let's go see what's on TV.

When Rachel wakes up it is daytime and she doesn't know why. Then she remembers the nurse and the big boy and then her tummy, except now her tummy doesn't hurt anymore so she is okay and she can get up.

Only she doesn't get up, because she sees on her wall

three bars of light that are dancing like someone is singing a song so she watches them dance forever. Then she really does hear someone singing only it's not singing it's talking. She hears Mommy's voice and then there's another voice. It's not Daddy. It's a voice she doesn't know.

Rachel thinks that maybe she is dreaming because this voice she doesn't know is scary like a dream so she closes her eyes. When she opens them again, she sees how when she holds her arm up just like this she can make the bars of light on the wall get smaller and if she holds up her other arm too then she can make them go away.

Rachel hears the man's voice and then she hears Mommy laugh. She puts her hands on the wall so the bars of light are dancing on her hands. Rachel makes her hands and the light dance together and sing and sing until she doesn't hear the voices anymore at all.

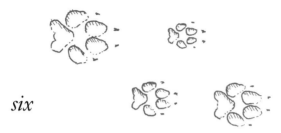

six

The coyote wisely makes himself inconspicuous whenever [a human] is about.

After Ralph left, Natalie settled in next to the cage. She could feel the coyote watching her. He didn't seem wary but curious.

What she really wanted to do was talk with him, but now that they were alone, she realized just how absurd this desire was. The coyote wouldn't understand her, wouldn't be able to respond. And what would she say? That she was sorry for her species' sorry history with his, sorry for the stalkings, the trappings, the killings? The coyote didn't care if she were sorry or not. Yet she was determined to let him know not all of her species were determined to destroy his.

She shifted slightly in the sand next to the cage so that they could look at each other. The coyote's eyes were a marvelous egg yolk yellow, rimmed in black as if he'd taken the time to apply eyeliner. There was enough about him that was dog-like that Natalie was wary, because she didn't trust dogs. At the same time, the resemblance made her certain the coyote possessed a native intelligence that was equally certain of hers.

As he studied her, his ears were as active as his eyes. One, she noted, was nicked about an inch below its point. How'd you hurt your ear? she asked him. She realized it was the first time she'd spoken.

The coyote's ears twitched at the sound. Then he tilted his head slightly to one side and watched her. Did you get it caught on a piece of barbed wire? she asked, encouraged by his attentiveness. Or did you and a sibling get a bit carried away when you were wrestling? The voice wasn't quite hers; it sounded the way some people's did when they talked to small children.

The coyote didn't answer, of course—had she thought (or hoped?) he would?—but he was listening. You can't trust people, she told him. I'm sure you already know that, but there's something else you should know, too. For everyone like me, who wants to coexist with you, there are fifty people who want you gone. And here's the saddest part. You won't win. I won't win. I'll keep trying and you'll keep trying, but man always prevails. And I do mean *man*.

She stopped speaking. Was this what she believed? Was this why she worked so hard to let people know that coyotes lived in Valle Bosque? Because she knew that someday they wouldn't? She realized there was something else she needed to tell the coyote, even though he couldn't understand a word she was saying.

As long as you and man covet the same territory, she said, he will try to kill you. He will not stop until every last one of you is dead. Peaceful coexistence is not an option. Sharing the same land is not an option. Reaching out to understand each other is not an option. You cannot understand each other. There is no common ground. There is no shared ground.

Natalie heard a pickup coming along the ditch road and looked up to see Ralph approaching in the old grey Ford half-ton. She realized she was crying again, and quickly pulled a tissue from her pocket and patted her eyes. Then she stood. She looked back down at the coyote, who continued to regard her with that same watchful gaze. I'm sorry, she said. I'm just one woman. I can't change a world of men.

But she would try, she thought. That's all I can promise you, she told the coyote. I'll try.

She hoped he understood that it wouldn't be enough.

To the editor:

You know, what's happening to Valle Bosque's coyotes isn't all that different from what happened to the Native Americans. No wonder someone cut the foot off the statue of Oñate at the Albuquerque Museum. I thought that was a grand gesture, to do the same thing Oñate himself did to the Acoma people he enslaved to build his mission church in the 16th century. Unlike Oñate's laborers', the statue's foot was returned. An interesting footnote, if you'll pardon my pun.

You might be wondering what this has got to do with coyotes. The thing is, the Native Americans, Hispanics, and the Anglos of New Mexico coexist a lot better than multicultural peoples do in other parts of the world. But sometimes, like with Oñate's foot, our old animosities bubble back to the surface. Here's what I see: conqueror after conqueror trying to tromp down those who were here before him (and I do mean "him"). Except the Native Americans couldn't be quashed. They retained their culture in spite of the most diligent efforts of those who conquered them, until finally, a few generations down the road, everyone just started getting along.

So that's what I'm talking about. Coyotes and people are a few generations down the road. Why not just try to get along? Stay out of each other's way, live and let live. Peacefully coexist, like Ms. Harold says. Like the Native Americans say, all that happens when you call someone your enemy is that he fights back. And sometimes, he wins.

Peace,

Redfern Goldstein

First, they watched Oprah. Neither one of them had ever watched Oprah before. Alison stretched out on the couch, and Sherman on the floor. At first uncomfortable with the vocal participation of the studio audience, Alison soon found herself tempted to lend her own amens to the chorus as a woman told the story of her abusive husband. One day, as the woman phrased it, she'd put her foot down and just walked away. In light of her courage, Alison forgave her the awkward metaphor.

Sherman, whenever she looked at him, seemed engrossed in the show, but there was no way to be sure. What Alison found most intriguing was his silence, the fact that, unlike Chris, he didn't seem to feel a need to fill every space with words. His lack of conversation kept her from making forays of her own. Instead, she found herself weighing every possible comment and finding it wanting.

Every few commercials, Alison tiptoed down the hall to check on Rachel, who continued to sleep soundly. When Oprah was over, Sherman stood up and stretched, then followed Alison down the hall and looked over her shoulder at the sleeping girl.

She looks just like you, he whispered.

Alison was surprised. She more often saw Chris in her daughter's features than herself. What do you mean? she asked, turning to look at him.

His face was very close to hers. She could see that he'd shaved that morning, and she wanted to touch the smoothness that she knew wouldn't last. She felt his breath on her forehead, smelled coffee and muffin and a lovely sweetness underneath that was his alone. The shape of her mouth, Sherman said. She has your mouth. He took a step back.

She wanted to step toward him, but stopped herself. She smiled. Oh no. This is my mouth—she touched her lips with her fingertips—that's hers. She gestured toward Rachel.

Sherman smiled. Of course. You're right. But you know what I mean. And her forehead. The shape of her face.

Alison had never parsed herself as Sherman was doing now. It was both thrilling and frightening to have someone pay such close attention. Do you suppose there's a cartoon on? she asked. Something horridly drawn, like Johnny Quest?

Johnny Quest! Did you watch Johnny Quest? I thought you were younger. Sherman's voice trailed off.

On cable. Old television programs never die; they just move to a different bandwidth. She wondered what difference her age made.

Sherman followed her back down the hall and into the living room, eased himself down to the floor again. You can sit on the couch, too, if you want, Alison said. There's plenty of room.

Sherman smiled and then joined her at the other end of the long sofa.

You can put your feet up on the coffee table, she told him. It's hooky day, remember?

He put his feet up. Then he put his hands behind his head and arched his back in a stretch. Alison took the opportunity to study his jaw, the place where his neck disappeared into the collar of his shirt. She again felt the urge to reach over, to touch the places she saw. Instead, she held the remote out toward him. Your turn, she said.

His fingers brushed hers as he took the remote. She felt a prickling, as if her hand had been long asleep. She dusted the fingers he'd touched with the palm of her other hand, made a circle, made the circle larger. Sherman was flipping through channels, stopped when he found a cartoon. They both watched for a moment to see what it was.

It's Cartoon Classics, Sherman said. I loved Cartoon

Classics when I was a boy. He turned and looked at her. This was pre–Johnny Quest, of course.

Alison had never heard of Cartoon Classics but she didn't say so. Instead, she tried to determine just what classic the cartoon on the screen was trying to depict. When she realized what it was, she laughed. Is it *Anna Karenina?* she asked. *Anna Karenina* for kids?

We were a sophisticated generation, Sherman said solemnly. It's only in our middle age that we've become childish. They both watched the screen for a few minutes. Cartoon Anna sat at her dressing table applying makeup. A cartoon maid who resembled the Disney Cinderella approached. Sherman and Alison both laughed when she spoke in Cinderella's voice.

So hard to keep one's classics pure, Sherman said.

So hard to keep anything pure, said Alison. Then she wondered for a brief moment what she meant. When she snuck a look at Sherman, she was relieved to see that he wasn't wondering. He was watching the cartoon. Alison tucked her feet beneath her and settled onto the couch more comfortably to do the same. The silence enveloped her like a comfort she'd been seeking all along.

Rachel can feel Mommy looking at her, but someone else is looking at her too. When he talks, Rachel knows it is the man from the voice in her dream. The voice is scary, so she pretends like she is sleeping so he will stop looking.

Rachel hears Mommy and the man talking some more, so she knows they are still here, but when she peeks through her eyes, she sees that they are not looking at her anymore. Then Mommy says, My mouth is hers, or something else Rachel doesn't understand. It gives her a funny fluttery feeling that is not her tummy ache. It doesn't hurt but she doesn't like it and it is the man that made it be there and Mommy that made the man be here. Mommy made Daddy get mad all the time so then he went away and that is Mommy's fault too, so then Rachel looks for the bars of light on the wall, but they are gone. Rachel wants that to be Mommy's fault, too, except that maybe it is really her own fault, because Rachel knows that maybe she made the bars of light go away just like she made Daddy go away, and this is why Mommy is so mad all the time, too. But if Rachel is very, very good then maybe this man will go away and Daddy will come back and she and Mommy and Daddy and Chris her coyote can all live happily ever after forever and ever.

Rachel decides that if she opens her eyes and the bars of light are there then this will all happen. But if the bars of light are not there when she opens her eyes then it will never happen, so she can only open her eyes when the bars of light *are* there. It makes her feel funny inside to know this and she hears how she is breathing like Mommy does sometimes. So then she decides if she opens one eye only a little it will not count as opening her eyes to make it not happen if the bars of light are not there. Slowly, slowly, she makes one of her eyes open just a little and *there they are!* So then she opens both of her eyes fast fast to make the magic work. She is so happy she puts both her hands in the bars of light and then her hands and the bars of light sing and dance together because they are so happy too.

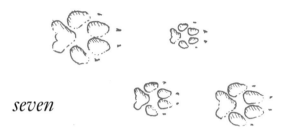

seven

The versatile coyote may have been forced to adapt himself to a more solitary life to survive the advance of civilization.

It was Natalie the coyote watched while Ralph dug out the cage and carried it to the pickup, Natalie it watched once Ralph had secured the cage and slammed the tailgate shut. Even after she and Ralph got back into the cab, Natalie could feel the animal's eyes on the back of her head, and when she turned, she saw it was watching her still.

The coyote seemed to want her to continue what she'd been saying, but of course to think that it had understood a word she'd said was absurd. Or was it? The usual dispassionate logic on which Natalie prided herself seemed to have abandoned her at the moment the coyote's eyes met hers. It was as if the coyote knew she was the best hope not just for him, but for his species, at least as far as Valle Bosque was concerned. It was as if the coyote knew that how he interacted with Natalie could have much larger repercussions than any connection he forged with Ralph.

But, she reminded herself, it was Ralph who would determine this coyote's fate. She hadn't made that clear to the coyote, she realized now. She'd been focusing on the bigger issue at the expense of the more immediate one. It was something she often did, jumping from the concrete to the abstract. Her ex-husband Keith had once said it was one of the things that first attracted him to her. She would now add that it was this same dispassion that contributed to their breakup.

The truth was, except for Sherman, briefly Keith, and now perhaps Ralph Sandoval, Natalie had a hard time connecting with people. She couldn't understand the way most insisted petty details were important while ignoring the much bigger picture those details masked. She couldn't understand—no, she didn't like—the way others wore their emotions on their not-always-very-clean sleeves, the way they offered themselves to each other as if the only puzzle were how you could fit two people together so the seams were invisible.

What had initially attracted Natalie to Keith was his dispassion, how, even if they disagreed, he could stand back and look at the altercation like a clinician studying the disagreement patterns of humans. A lot of women wouldn't like that kind of removal, but it was precisely what Natalie had desired, a sort of narrative distance that was at the same time exact and honest and clear. She was certain his future patients would value it as well.

Back then, Natalie believed that a relationship based on dispassion would last far longer than one with a passionate origin, but she'd been wrong. By the time Keith had finished his residency, he was insisting Natalie explore the origin of what he'd begun to call her emotional disconnect. While Keith continued to keep an emotional distance from his patients, he said he had learned the importance of emotional connection in his primary relationships.

Natalie couldn't begin to imagine how she might learn to forge such a connection. For one thing, the things that made her cry were not the things that made other people cry. She'd cried twice just now, for example, because the coyote was in a cage, but it wasn't because her heart, so to speak, went out to the coyote. She'd cried because of how unnatural it was, because it didn't fit with how things ought to be. It was the same way she felt when someone attacked her in yet another letter to the editor of the *Valle Bosque Beacon*. She didn't feel threatened; she was frustrated that the letter writers refused to see what to her was as clear as desert air.

That was what Natalie liked about coyotes. In fact, that was what struck her about this particular coyote. She could still feel him watching her now as Ralph eased the pickup from the dirt track along the ditch bank onto the paved feeder road that led to Valle Bosque's main street. Coyotes didn't strive to match their perceptions to their preconceptions. They used what they saw to create a reality that changed depending on what they saw. Every situation was unique. Unlike humans, Natalie thought, coyotes were adaptable. Thinking that, she felt as if she'd stumbled onto something that had up until then been just out of her reach. But as soon as she touched it, it was gone.

Natalie refocused her attention on the present, then realized they were headed north instead of south, away from the village center instead of toward it. Where are we going? she asked Ralph.

We need to set him free, Ralph said, not taking his eyes from the road. There's this place I know up along the Rio Puerco. He looked quickly in Natalie's direction and then away.

What had she been expecting? That they'd lock the coyote into one of the cages in the back room of the village offices? That she could take it home and keep it, in this cage, perhaps, out on her *portal*? She hadn't thought it through at all. Now that she did, she saw that Ralph was right.

Still, it was springtime. If this coyote were part of a pack, he'd be missed. Natalie turned to look at him over her shoulder. He continued to focus on her and for a moment she returned his calm gaze. He was young. Chances were, he was still solitary and hadn't yet mated. It was a good time to move him, she thought. She shifted back around and then looked over at Ralph. Will you get in trouble? she asked him.

I'll write it up, he said. I think Frank'll be happy to have this problem disappear.

But it's only one. Will you do it again and again, every time you catch a coyote?

Ralph braked for the signal where the road met the four-lane state highway, then turned to look at her. He smiled. That's my plan, he said. What do you think?

Natalie—not a woman to whom touching came easily—reached up to lightly touch Ralph's arm where it stretched across the back of the seat. I think you are a brilliant and resourceful man, Ralph Sandoval.

Still smiling, Ralph nodded. That's what I thought, too. But it's good to hear you say it. Then he eased the truck out onto the highway that would lead them toward the Jemez Mountains.

To the editor:

Well, I never thought I'd be one to agree with one of those Indian wannabe hippies. Usually, they've got their heads stuck so far in the ground, their butts are all that's showing. It's nice to read something from one that makes sense for a change. That Redfeather Goldman [Editor's note: Mr. Curtis is referring to Redfern Goldstein] got it exactly right. "When you call someone your enemy . . .he fights back. And sometimes, he wins." So I say, again, may the best man win.

Jim Curtis

Alison noted how Sherman had stretched out still more comfortably, as if sitting on her couch in the middle of the day to watch cartoons were something he did all the time. But she'd never done anything like this before, she thought, her eyes unfocused on cartoon Anna Karenina and her growing dilemma.

She'd never even really dated anyone but Chris. Dated? Was this a date? What *was* a date? What a foolish word, as if it were the moment and not the relationship that mattered. But then Alison was behaving foolishly. Just down the hall, her seven-year-old daughter lay ill and asleep, and what was she doing? She was entertaining a near stranger in her living room.

She stole yet another look at Sherman. He didn't look like a stranger. More important, he didn't *feel* like a stranger. He felt, in fact, like someone she'd known a very long time. Maybe it was the companionable silence. Maybe it was the way he'd settled into her house as if it were somewhere he already knew. Whatever the reason, Alison felt comfortable with Sherman in a way she'd never felt with another man. She'd never even felt that way with Chris, if she were honest with herself. High school had added them together as if there were a mathematical formula to determine it: quarterback + cheerleader = couple. Everyone just assumed they belonged together, and so they had. Everyone just assumed they'd get married, and so they'd done that, too. Everyone just assumed… But what about *her*? Hadn't she been willing to ride along on those assumptions? Hadn't it been simple to not take responsibility for her life, but to instead let others determine it? And wasn't that, just maybe, why she was so angry with Chris, for forcing her to have to take some responsibility?

Alison felt her fists clench, but compelled herself to continue. After all, Chris had been the other part of the equation, and he'd coasted along, too, for all those years. No, Chris hadn't coasted, though that may have been how it appeared to others. Alison allowed herself the rare indulgence of investigating for a moment his always-unexpected stellate anger, its sharp points like barbs that tore through her skin in a way no real object could. She thought about the mix of fear and—yes, if she were honest were herself—exquisite and nearly sexual tension she felt at those moments Chris inexplicably exploded. Later, she'd go back over what she'd said or done that had led to that moment, compare it to the ones that had come before. But there were never any parallels that she could see, nor was there a map, either to guide or to warn her.

And yet it was that very dangerous and unknown aspect of Chris that had both attached her to him and made the fact of Didi so surprising. Surely Chris didn't want someone else to know his—their—secret. Surely the fact that Alison had never told cemented their bond. She wondered if he had progressed to his particular brand of verbal violence with Didi yet. She wondered what Didi would do when she met it.

Then again, maybe Chris had simply seen what he and Alison were really about sooner than Alison had. Maybe when he met Didi he had realized there was more to life than coasting—and sometimes, not coasting. Maybe when he met Didi, he felt exactly the way Alison was feeling right now, with Sherman Gold sitting next to her on the couch. Alison felt such a rush of what must have been forgiveness flood her that she was tempted to call Chris right this minute and tell him that she understood. Then she considered Rachel and how their break-up had affected her, was still affecting her, and just as quickly felt the forgiveness melt away, the anger return.

Ultimately, that had been the real nature of Alison and Chris's relationship: anger and forgiveness, fury and apology. Like a child on a swing who depended on someone else to push her, Alison could never be quite certain just how

Lisa Lenard-Cook

hard Chris might shove. There was in fact the same thrilling mix of elation and fear, but this wasn't something she'd ever told anyone else either.

Alison was reminded of another thing she'd never told: that she had always secretly believed that she'd been at fault those times Chris had exploded, that she'd said something she shouldn't have said, or done something she shouldn't have done. More than once Chris had called her a manipulative bitch, and, really, when she thought about it, she could see why he'd think that. She didn't do it intentionally. She didn't even do it mindfully; but she could look back at those moments and see precisely how the thing she'd said or done had (as Chris would have phrased it if it were something they ever discussed) put him over the edge.

But it wasn't something they ever discussed. And it wasn't something that anyone else knew, either. Not even Molly. Thinking of her friend led Alison to picture Molly nodding her approval at Alison sitting here on her couch with Sherman Gold in the middle of the day. Alison smiled at the nodding Molly, then realized that Sherman Gold was watching her. How long had he been? On the television, *Anna Karenina* was gone, her place taken by an aging and plasticized former sitcom star demonstrating some monstrosity of an exercise device. Alison tried to figure it out and quickly gave up. She could feel Sherman still watching her. She needed to say something. She couldn't think of a thing.

When she turned to look at him, he didn't shift his gaze at all. He just kept watching her. What was he thinking? That she was pretty? Is that what he was thinking? Was he thinking that he wanted to kiss her? Did she want him to?

102

Alison became aware of the way her heart reverberated against her ribs, the way her collarbone lifted when she breathed in, lowered when she breathed out. Say something, Alison, she commanded herself. Say anything.

Anna Karenina? she managed.

Once again departed beneath the rails of the train, Sherman said. They didn't show it, of course. It was left it open to allusion—a shoe abandoned on a platform, the train whistling off into its tunnel. Less imaginative children might be left to think that Anna got on the train wearing only one shoe.

Or more imaginative children, Alison said. The word children made her think again of Rachel and she stood. Her knees and ankles hurt from having been curled onto them for so long, and she pointed her toes before gesturing toward the hallway. I'll be right back, she said.

Are you hungry? Sherman asked. I can make us some lunch.

As soon as he asked, Alison realized she was. I can do that, she said.

Sherman stood. No. No. I like to cook. I like to cook in other people's kitchens especially. As long as you don't mind me poking around your cupboards.

His words caused Alison to picture something quite different from Sherman poking around her cupboards. She pictured Sherman poking around her body, exploring every inch of it. The idea sent a shiver through her. Poke away, she managed, before escaping down the hall to the safety of Rachel's room.

*　　　*　　　*

Ralph turned northwest on the highway formerly known as 44. Natalie had been this way before, of course, but this time she focused on the landscape as a home for the coyote who watched alertly from his cage in the back of the pickup. Once they'd topped the sandbrown mesa that rose from the Rio Grande Valley, nothing lay between them and the black Jemez Mountains but the red hills that skirted them. The four-lane highway unwound between the Indian pueblos that lined the dry gulch of the Rio Jemez. Did you have somewhere in mind? Natalie asked Ralph.

Matter of fact, I do, Ralph said. There's old land grant territory up past San Ysidro. Figure we'll drive in a ways and then set our friend loose.

Natalie recalled that the Spanish settlers of New Spain had received the land grants in the sixteenth century, each large plot a reward for services to the king. That the land was not the king's to grant was not a possibility either the settlers or the king considered, and contemporary old timers often bemoaned the theft of this same land by the Anglos who arrived 300 years later.

But no one can own this land, Natalie thought now. Not really. And yet the battles over the endless expanses of mountain and mesa went on, as did the battles for what little water traversed them. In fact, as the altitude increased, the drought winter's effect became ever more apparent. In other Aprils, the Rio Jemez would be swollen with snowmelt and the hillsides green after their winter undercover. This year, the only green was provided by the random dots of sagebrush scattered across the hills, and it wasn't a lush green but a tired and resigned one.

Ralph slowed the pickup through the tiny village of San Ysidro then sped up again on the newly widened highway that continued north to Cuba. Fifteen minutes later, he slowed again before turning left onto a dirt track that crossed the dry riverbed on a suspect one-lane bridge then pointed toward the distinctive profile of El Cabezon. The singular butte was a lonely sentinel over its corner of the high desert, a landmark for hundreds of surrounding miles.

Ralph steered carefully but drove faster than Natalie felt he should on such a road, and she held tightly to the armrest that rattled on the door. In the back of the pickup, the coyote's cage shuddered and bounced, but inside it the coyote sat calmly. Watching.

The sun, almost directly overhead, made Natalie aware it must be close to noon. She was hungry, she realized. But with San Ysidro growing ever more distant in the dust behind them, she knew she wouldn't be eating for a while. She should have thought to ask Ralph to stop. But wouldn't he be hungry, too?

Well, why not ask? She turned to Ralph. Can I buy you lunch after we're done?

Oh, said Ralph. I've got a couple burritos packed here. Well, shoot, we should of stopped and got something for you, huh? Tell you what. I'll let you have one of my burritos and then you can buy me an ice cream sandwich when we roll back through San Ysidro. I'm a sucker for ice cream sandwiches.

Natalie almost said, Oh that's all right, I'm not hungry, but she stopped herself. She *was* hungry. And Ralph had just offered her a burrito in exchange for an ice cream sandwich. It was probably the best offer she'd get all day.

That's the best offer I've had all day, she said, and Ralph laughed.

Behind them, the coyote sat in his cage. Soon, Natalie told him in her mind. Soon you'll be home. Soon you'll be free. How she envied him his good fortune. How she envied him his adaptability and innate skills. Give it up, Nat, Sherman would say when they were children and she'd shared sentiments like these. No, she answered him now. This dream is all mine.

When Mommy stands by Rachel's bed she makes it dark on Rachel's face. How you feeling, Mommy says, and Rachel says she is hungry, can she have something to eat. Well, that's a good sign, Mommy says. I have a friend here who will make you lunch.

Rachel thinks it is Molly, but then Mommy says his name is Sherman, and Rachel thinks what a funny name that is, Sure-man. Then she remembers the scary man she dreamed except now she thinks that maybe she didn't dream him. Does Daddy know? she asks Mommy, and then she is sorry she said that because Mommy's shoulders pull up that way they do. What's Daddy got to do with it? she asks before she makes her shoulders go down again like she didn't just get all mad. Well let's get you up and around if you're hungry, she says, and Rachel thinks that she doesn't like this man, this Sure-man, who thinks he can just come along, even when nobody even asked him and nobody wants him and his name isn't even Chris, and think that he can make somebody lunch.

When Rachel gets to the kitchen, this man is standing

at the stove with a towel tucked into his pants like Mommy makes Rachel do sometimes when she is eating sketty. When he turns around he sees Rachel and smiles and says hello and then goes back to what he is doing at the stove. He doesn't kneel down like Uncle Tony. He doesn't say, Well, well, well, who have we here? like the man where Mommy works. He doesn't say, You must be Rachel, or, How old are you? or, You look just like your Mommy, or any of those other things that grownups say. He just goes back to what he is doing at the stove. It makes Rachel want to go see what he is doing so she pushes her chair over next to him and then climbs up to watch.

In the pan are dancing things like peas and carrots and apples and raisins. Rachel watches them jump around in the pan when the man shakes it and then she tells him, You can't put apples and raisins with peas and carrots. Oh, he says. Nobody ever told me that. What do you think will happen?

Rachel has to think about this. She knows that you can't put apples and raisins with peas and carrots, but she doesn't know why not. She looks at Mommy, who will know the answer, but she is putting plates on the table and doesn't see Rachel looking at her. Rachel looks back at the dancing peas and carrots and apples and raisins. They smell good.

Can I taste it? she asks the man. He slides a piece of apple and a piece of carrot onto his stirring spoon and then blows on them and holds them out to her. You can't eat off the cooking spoon, Rachel tells him. Nobody ever told me that either, he says. He is still holding the spoon out so Rachel looks over at Mommy's back and then pulls the pieces off the spoon with her teeth.

She likes the way the apple and carrot taste together. They are sweet, like candy, only it is almost better than candy. Now she sees there is another pot on the stove with a lid on it. What's in that pot? she asks Sherman. She has decided it is okay to think of him this way.

Rice, he says. You want to taste that, too? Mommy turns around then and looks right at Sherman and then right at Rachel and the way she smiles is like something Rachel remembers but knows has never happened before. Sherman is holding out the spoon with some rice on it and Mommy is still smiling so Rachel puts her teeth around the end of the spoon and eats the rice and Mommy doesn't say a word! She just keeps on smiling like a Mommy Rachel has never seen before.

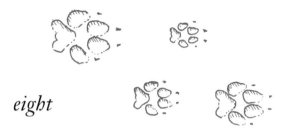

eight

COYOTE DEN DESTROYED

by *Tom Sullivan*, Beacon *editor*

Valle Bosque Animal Control Director Frank Sebold told the Beacon *Tuesday that a coyote den near the river was recently destroyed, along with six pups, after being discovered by a resident riding a horse along the bosque. The resident asked to remain anonymous.*

"It's within our power," Sebold said, "and we've got to do something to nip this thing in the bud. If some people don't like it, well, then, that's their problem."

Coyote Intelligence founder Natalie Harold cited several studies that she said suggest that when the coyote population is artificially decreased the animals reproduce more quickly. "Killing pups doesn't solve the problem,"

Harold said, "and may in fact exacerbate it. Understanding that coyotes live here just as we do is a far better solution."

Harold suggested that people who encounter coyotes scare them off. "If we make the animals aware that people are their enemy, they will be less likely to approach when humans are nearby. A big part of the current problem in the village is that the coyotes have decided that humans are not a threat."

When read Ms. Harold's comments, villager Jim Curtis, a vocal coyote opponent, said it sounds as if she might be "on the same page" as him after all. "I'll show them a threat," Curtis said. "Right down the barrel of my ought-six. Coyotes are killers, plain and simple. This is my property, and if I see a coyote trespassing, I'll do what I have to, to protect it."

Some villagers have advocated using humane traps and then releasing the coyotes in other areas, such as on Bureau of Land Management or National Forest land, but many experts believe trapped-and-released animals could end up in rival territories and be destroyed by their own kind. Animal Control Director Sebold said that although trap-and-release has been tried with some success in other New Mexico cities and towns, he did not endorse such a plan.

Sebold noted that there has been an increased number of human-coyote encounters this spring. "It could be the dry winter," he said. "Coyotes survive by adapting to changed conditions, and if finding food during a drought means becoming bolder with humans, that's what they'll do. The acre-plus spreads we've got *here in Valle Bosque probably look like Furr's [Cafeteria] to them."*

With the increase in human-coyote encounters, some villagers have expressed concern that the animals may attack their children, but so far no attacks have been reported. Animal Control keeps a log of all coyote encounters. Villagers who wish to make a report should call the village offices.

Natalie remembered from her reading that, given the opportunity, trapped coyotes sometimes attacked the man who trapped them. Some would bide their time, the article had said, referring to a coyote's patience as one of its virtues. This related to steel traps, of course, not the more humane cage Ralph had used. Still, she wondered if the coyote in the back of the pickup was in fact biding its time, so she asked Ralph, who, with one casual hand on the wheel, was steering the pickup along the ruts that passed for a road.

It's possible, Ralph said. I don't know. Not many people do coyote catch-and-release, and if they do, they're not letting anyone else know. Most folks just kill 'em straight out.

I appreciate what you're doing, Natalie said.

We'll see, said Ralph. And listen. When I do open up that cage, I want you in the cab of the pickup. With the door closed. And I'll have my shotgun ready, just in case. I don't want you to be surprised or upset if I have to use it.

All right, she said.

The interior of the cab darkened momentarily as the road passed through a narrow slot, and then they came out into what would have been a meadow in a wetter year. Today, it was just another dry expanse of pale green sage and grey chamisa, stretching toward the towering presence that was El Cabezon. Ralph stopped the truck without pulling off the track and then shut it off. Its engine continued to tick for a moment, and in the side mirror Natalie watched the dust the tires had kicked up settle back into the two dirt ruts that marked the dwindling perspective of the path they'd taken. Nothing else stirred.

Well, Ralph said after a minute. Now or never, I guess. He opened his door and hopped down, then reached behind the seat to take his shotgun down from the gun rack. When Natalie turned to watch him, she saw that the coyote was watching, too, and when Ralph cracked the gun open, the coyote's ears lowered forward. It growled once, low and menacing.

It knows what a shotgun is, said Natalie.

Well then, if it's so smart, it'll know enough to not make me use it. Does he think I'd drive him all this way just to kill him?

The coyote growled again.

Ralph, Natalie said. I think you shouldn't be holding onto the shotgun when you go out there.

Ralph laughed, one short syllable. I may be a lot of things, he said, but I ain't stupid.

It would be stupid to be holding the gun when you opened the cage, she persisted. The coyote doesn't like the gun.

I didn't bring you out here to argue with me, Ralph said. Natalie heard something new in his voice. She wondered if Nina heard this sometimes, too. She thought of how Nina would react, and then of what Nina might say.

I'm not arguing with you, she said when she knew. I'm trying to convince you of the best thing to do. I've been researching coyote behavior a long time, Ralph. I wish you would trust me.

I *do* trust you. Hell, would I of brought you if I didn't trust you?

Then put down the gun, Ralph. Natalie heard echoes of old westerns when she said it. Please. For me. She hoped her voice didn't sound whiny. She hoped it sounded like Nina's would, strong and self-assured.

Ralph looked through the back window at the coyote, who returned his gaze without blinking. Its ears were still lowered, but it didn't growl when their eyes met. Ralph lifted the gun into the coyote's sight-range experimentally and then the coyote did growl. Hunh, Ralph said. How 'bout that. He didn't unload the gun, but he did set it back in the rack. Remind me to unload before we start back or one of us could end up with a hole in the head.

I'll remind you, said Natalie. She looked back at the coyote. His ears were once more alert and questioning, and she knew then that she'd been right.

To the editor:

People have been stopping me at the post office and the village grocery, in the mercantile and the school, even when I'm out on the bosque riding. Everyone's asking if I'm the one who reported that den of coyote pups that was destroyed by Animal Control. They figure it must have been me because I wrote that letter about Banjo.

Even my kids are mad at me. Bobby, my youngest, was crying. "They were babies," he said. "How could you?" When I told him it wasn't me, he didn't believe me.

But I really wasn't the one who reported the den. *Since so many people think I was, though, I thought about what I would have done if I would have been the one who found it. And you know what?* I would *have reported it. But the things people have said to me, the way people have assumed it* was *me, the way everyone seems so divided, either for the coyotes or against them, made me think some more. Why is it that everyone feels so strongly about the coyotes, whether they're for them, like Mrs. Harold, or against them, like Jim Curtis? I wondered if maybe I was missing something.*

That was when I remembered that coyote education booklet the village mailed out a few months back. I know it was Natalie Harold who got that to happen, but even though I didn't read it at the time, for some reason I dropped it in my junk drawer instead of just throwing it away. Now that I've read it, I can say I'm glad I hung onto it. It turns out it's not junk at all.

First of all, it doesn't recommend going out and hugging your neighborhood coyote, like Mrs. Harold's critics say she would have us all doing if she got her way. What the pamphlet does say is that the coyotes are not going to go away, no matter what we do, so the best thing we can do is make it clear to them that *we're* not going away either, and that they'd better steer clear of us.*

The pamphlet lists all sorts of ways we can let the coyotes know they should be afraid of us. Throwing rocks, for example, or shouting. It doesn't come out and blame the people who don't fence their livestock if a coyote gets one of their animals, which is another thing I thought it said before I read it. But it does "recommend" enclosed pens, and guard animals like llamas, donkeys, and large dogs.

What struck me most of all, though, was where it said, "Coyotes are opportunistic animals." Just like humans, I thought. Suddenly it all fell into place. If humans did what the coyotes are doing, we might call them brave, you know? Just struggling to survive. But instead, we see them as an enemy. I see them as my enemy. One ate Banjo, after all, and my kids loved that rooster.

But now I'm thinking it's like that hippie said: When you call someone your enemy, of course he'll fight back. It's human nature to fight back when someone attacks you. So are the coyotes our enemy because we see them that way, or are we the coyotes' enemy? You see what I mean? Maybe, like one of my kids' teachers says, we need to get to the root of the problem before we can solve it.

Yours truly,

Kathy Crawford

The conversation Rachel and Sherman carried on during lunch left Alison an observer, but the role allowed her the leisure to observe both without appearing obvious. She noted how Sherman addressed Rachel as an equal rather than as a child, and how Rachel responded in kind, as if it were the way she routinely conducted her conversations.

Alison was both surprised and pleased at this Rachel she didn't know and hadn't suspected existed. The surprise was that Rachel was being brought out by a stranger, a man who wasn't Chris. It had been Alison's observation that Rachel didn't like men, although until now it hadn't occurred to Alison to be concerned about it. Now she wondered why she did like this one.

Maybe she liked Sherman for the same reasons Alison did, which of course insisted that Alison consider just what it was about Sherman Gold, other than his extraordinary good looks, that attracted her. His ease, she thought, how he's so natural, unassuming, immediately comfortable. She felt as if this weren't quite it, as if she needed to pinpoint what she was looking for. She tuned into Sherman and Rachel's conversation again.

Chris would move in with us but he's a coyote, Rachel was saying.

Coyotes don't much like living in houses, said Sherman, nodding his agreement. Of course, there are times when I don't like living in houses, either.

Me, too, said Rachel. She spooned some food into her mouth and chewed thoughtfully. Alison noted that her plate was more than half empty. That was something, too. Rachel swallowed, then spoke again. Maybe I could live with Chris outside sometimes, she said.

Sherman thought about this for a moment before answering. He probably lives in a culvert, he said, or a hole somewhere. He probably poops right on his doorstep.

Rachel giggled, a seven-year-old girl again. Yuck! she cried. Sherman looked Alison's way and smiled.

Alison smiled back at him, felt again the still-unidentifiable sensation. Was this what the beginning of love felt like? she wondered. She couldn't remember. But then, maybe she'd never been here before. Maybe that was why she couldn't narrow down what it was about Sherman that attracted her. Wasn't love blind, after all?

What did it mean, that love was blind? Alison suddenly recalled the college English professor who had insisted on deconstructing not just every book but every word and phrase. At the time, Alison had found it tiresome, but as she'd gotten older, she'd discovered that decoding a phrase's meaning sometimes offered her a key to understanding the situation that had made her think of the phrase in the first place.

So: Love is blind. When we make decisions emotionally, we don't see clearly. Alison sat back, stunned. Was she making decisions emotionally? She looked again at Sherman Gold, who was once more talking to Rachel, this time about desserts. If love was blind, this was her just dessert, Alison thought. But desserts were the frosting on the cake. God, Alison. She smiled at herself, refocused on the table, and then on Rachel and Sherman.

Welcome back, Sherman said. Where were you this time?

Alison considered telling him the trajectory of her thoughts, then remembered she'd begun with love is blind. Just desserts, she said. Frosting on the cake.

Can we have cake? Rachel asked.

Alison recalled that there was a carrot cake in the freezer. Yes, we can, she said. And frosting, too.

A just dessert, said Sherman, smiling. Enough deconstruction, Alison decided. It's time for the here and now.

*   *   *

Here goes nothing, Ralph said. After donning heavy work gloves, he'd lowered the tailgate and hopped up into the truck bed. Now he stood next to the cage. Both the door of the cage and Ralph faced the rear of the truck.

Natalie had kneeled backward in her seat to watch. She felt as if she were seven years old again, peering through winter fog toward the street below. Unlike then, she had no need to imagine what she couldn't see. Still, in its way, what she was observing now was no less dreamlike.

Ralph reached down toward the cage experimentally. The coyote didn't lunge. It didn't even move. It just watched attentively. As smart as Natalie knew coyotes were, she was nonetheless awed by this one's seeming understanding of the situation. Because surely he understood, she thought. Surely he knew that Ralph meant to set him free. Why else, she thought again, would they have driven him all this way? Coyotes were capable of deduction. The more she saw of this one, the more she was certain this was so.

Now that Ralph had determined that the coyote wasn't going to attack him, he reached slowly for the bar release that topped the door. The coyote watched, but didn't move. The moment elongated, and Natalie felt the hairs on the back of her neck stand on end. She willed the coyote to turn and look at her one more time, but it seemed to know in which direction freedom lay. Natalie thought she saw its muscles tense, a prelude to action, but maybe she only imagined it.

As she watched, Ralph turned the bar and then flipped it up in one swift motion. The door sprang open. The coyote launched out, not even grazing the tailgate. Then it ran. It didn't turn. It didn't slow. Its receding pouf of dust grew smaller and smaller and then, all too soon, was gone.

Ralph and Natalie watched the place where the coyote had disappeared for what seemed like a very long time but was probably only seconds. Then Ralph turned to Natalie. Well that was easy, he said. You ready for lunch?

2003: Coyote Tracking Log

Date	Time	Location	Incident Reported
4/9/03	12:30 p.m.	BLM – San Ysidro District	released 2 yr old male

If Sherman lived here with her and Mommy, every day Rachel could eat carrots and apples together and taste things from the cooking spoon. Sherman says funny things to make Rachel laugh, like that coyotes poop on their doors and sleep in dirty holes in the ground, and he doesn't act like Chris is not her coyote. It is like he knows how it is.

When Rachel finishes eating then Sherman says, Well, Miss Rachel, do you want to wash or dry? I don't know how to wash *or* dry, she tells him, so he says, In that case you will dry, and he pulls her special kitchen chair next to the sink and then gives her a towel. Rachel looks at Mommy because she doesn't want her to be mad, but it is like Mommy is a new person who will never be mad again. I have a dishwasher, Mommy says.

So you do, says Sherman, and he rolls up his sleeves. And a dishdryer, too. Are you ready, Miss Rachel?

I am ready, Mr. Sherman, Rachel says, and then she waits to see what will happen next.

nine

Coyote Facts

Habitat: Coyotes are highly adaptable and can exist in various habitats such as deserts, swamps, mountain ranges, tropical, arctic, brush and grasslands. Coyotes have also adapted to living in densely populated areas such as New York City, Los Angeles and other large cities.

Natalie and Ralph sat on the tailgate, legs dangling toward the ground. All that remained of Ralph's burritos were their foil wrappers. The noon sun warmed what otherwise would have been a cool day and Natalie basked gratefully in its yellow heat.

Her eyes were drawn again and again to the horizon point at which the coyote had disappeared. She'd never seen anything run that way, she thought. It was as if it not only knew where it were going, but meant to arrive there as soon as it could. And yet the coyote had had no idea where it was going. How could it?

But there was so much it *had* seemed to know. Natalie was certain. She pictured again the way it had watched her while she'd talked to it back in Valle Bosque, a moment she now lingered over in order to capture every detail in her memory so that she could return whenever she chose. She felt again the way it had watched her while they had driven here, to this place she had never been before and would now always cherish.

She turned to Ralph. Thank you for bringing me, she said.

De nada, Ralph answered. Like her, he looked off toward where the coyote had disappeared. It's something, setting a coyote free.

His phrasing made Natalie think this wasn't the first time. Have you done this before? she asked.

Ralph turned to look at her, then smiled. I guess I can trust you, he said.

Natalie smiled back. I guess you'd better.

Ralph nodded, then looked off again. At least once a week, he said.

Surprise slapped her like an sudden wind. Once a week! For how long?

Ralph thought about it. Since fall, maybe?

Natalie could feel every heartbeat. That's, what, twenty coyotes you've relocated?

Ralph nodded again. More or less, I guess.

Seeds of tears pooled yet again. And why? Because Ralph was quietly and without ceremony making things better for both the coyote and human populations of Valle Bosque. *Tzedaka*, that was what it was called. Natalie hadn't thought of this Hebrew term in years. It meant charity, but of a particular kind: The best *Tzedaka* was anonymous. She thought about trying to explain this to Ralph, but realized he likely didn't know she was Jewish. It wasn't something she hid, but it wasn't necessarily something she revealed either. And it wasn't that it mattered, exactly; it was more that it shouldn't, but usually did. Rather than discover something she didn't want to see in Ralph, she chose to not mention *Tzedaka* at all. Still, she had to let him know how marvelous what he was doing was, how affirming, how *brave*.

It's good, what you're doing, she said.

Ralph shrugged his shoulders. It's no big deal.

No, said Natalie. It *is* a big deal. If more people quietly followed their consciences, just think how much better a world this would be.

Oh, I dunno. I think most people *do* follow their consciences, like you say. It's just that everyone's conscience is telling 'em something different. Someone else might think it was right to shoot every one of those coyotes for killing chickens and cats and such, and he'd be just as right in his way as I am in mine.

If it had been about anything else but coyotes,, Natalie might have agreed. Why do you do it, then? she asked him. What makes you someone who sets them free rather than shoots them?

Ralph's eyes remained on the horizon. I expect it has something to do with those Vietnamese pigs, he said. Not that that makes a whole lot of sense. He jumped off the tailgate as if for emphasis and landed easily on two feet, then turned to help her down.

It *does* make sense, said Natalie, jumping down quickly and awkwardly, but without his help. Maybe, she told herself, they *did* agree. Maybe they just had different ways of saying the same thing. She knew as she thought this that it probably wasn't so, but rather than dwell on their differences, she forced herself back into the moment. I owe you an ice cream sandwich, she said, opening the passenger door.

Ralph had unloaded the shotgun and set it back in its rack and was now cranking the truck's engine. Sounds like an offer I can't refuse, he said. Then the engine caught, and Ralph backed the truck expertly through the sand and shifted gears before beginning to retrace their course along the twin dirt tracks back toward San Ysidro.

It was as if Rachel had never been ill. On any other day, Alison might have taken her back to school and returned to work, but this was hardly any other day. She wondered if Sherman would stay or go, wondered whether she should ask him his plans or simply ask him to stay.

Rachel solved her dilemma by asking Sherman if he

liked to play Candy Land. I don't believe I've ever played Candy Land, Sherman answered.

Rachel cast him a look of disbelief. *Everybody* plays Candy Land, she told him. Even *Daddy* played Candy Land, when he was a little boy.

Over the top of Rachel's head, Sherman sent Alison an amused smile. I hope you can help me rectify this unfortunate gap in my education, he said to Rachel.

Rachel tilted her head to one side. Alison was about to translate when Rachel spoke. I can try, she said. But I can't make any guarantees. Alison stifled her urge to laugh at the echo of her own phrasing.

Rachel pulled the box from under the couch and carefully laid the game elements on the coffee table while Alison and Sherman watched. I'll be green, she told Sherman. You'll be blue. When she didn't assign Alison a game piece, Alison realized that she hadn't been asked to play.

I should feel slighted, she thought, but she didn't. It occurred to her that she could use this opportunity to go for a run, something she'd not done now for two mornings. But wouldn't it be an imposition to ask Sherman to watch Rachel while she did? It wasn't as if he'd come over to play Candy Land with her daughter.

Why *had* Sherman come over? Alison wondered. Yes, she'd said she wanted to see the poem, but then? For the first time since his arrival, she felt a gnaw of doubt about his motives. Who *was* this man, anyway? Why had she allowed him so easily into her house and her life? And Rachel's life, for that matter?

Alison took a figurative step away from herself and considered Sherman Gold. Why was he here? What did he want from her? More to the point, what did *she* want from *him*? Companionship? Sex? A new relationship to replace the old? But the old was barely over. Well then, why not be more like Molly? Alison's breath caught as she considered the possibility. What did that mean, to be more like Molly?

It meant being sure of herself, for one thing. It meant not needing a man to complete her. It meant that she should consider what she wanted at this very moment, not what Sherman wanted, not even what Rachel wanted. You go, girl! urged the Molly in her head, echoing Oprah's audience. Do something for yourself for a change.

Alison watched as Rachel showed Sherman how Candy Land was played. Sherman listened closely, nodded solemnly. Nothing in his demeanor suggested an ulterior motive. Nothing about him suggested that he wasn't simply a man who liked her, and liked Rachel, too. All those years with Chris had made her suspicious of ulterior motives, Alison thought. It was time for her to learn to trust people, or at least to trust this one person. And it was time for her to do something for herself.

Would you mind if I went for a run? she asked. She wasn't certain if she were asking Rachel or Sherman, but it was Rachel who answered.

Go ahead, she said, not looking up from the board.

Above Rachel's head, Sherman met Alison's eyes again. Go, he mouthed. Then he smiled. For some reason, Alison thought of the coyote, then realized why. It was because Rachel had named the coyote Chris, as if she knew where danger lay better than Alison, as if she knew her own father posed more of a threat than this smiling stranger. No: Not a stranger. Not anymore. *Trust*, Alison told herself. Then, with a nod to Sherman, she rose and went to change into her running clothes.

To the editor:

Mrs. Crawford is right. People who live in Valle Bosque should try to discover the root of their problem with the coyotes without killing each other off. It is for this reason that I thought it might help to share what the Indians of Tamaya Pueblo do. We may be only a few miles up the river, but we are in many ways a world removed from you.

Indians and coyotes have been sharing the same places for as long as Indians can remember, and this sharing has not always been an easy one, for us or for the coyotes. But Indians do not rush to solutions. First, we study the problem from every side. We do this for a long time, so we do not miss a side. Where you might say that every problem has two sides, Indians believe you cannot know how many sides a problem has until you have discovered and examined them all.

"What do we have that coyote wants?" we ask. "And what does coyote have that we want?" The answer to the first question includes our goats and lambs and chickens, but also our corn and frijoles *and even, sometimes, our chiles. The answer to the second question is his stealth and cunning, coyote's way of appearing where we do not know he is and just as quickly disappearing again.*

So then, we think, if we offer coyote what he wants that is ours, perhaps he will offer us what we want that is his. This is why, long ago, our ancestors made a special time and place to give coyote his share of our food. They set out a fresh-slaughtered lamb, some ground corn, a bowl of frijoles. *Into the night, the dancers danced and the singers sang, "We share these things with you, coyote, that you may share your ways with us." This is something the Indians continue to do, although sometimes it is hamburger we set out rather than lamb, and sometimes the hamburger comes from McDonald's or Burger King.*

But what has the white man given coyote? Here is a story we tell about this:

One time a crow in a tree and a coyote on the ground under him were having a conversation, full of wisdom. This did not keep the crow from looking around.

Presently he said, "Right now we shall have to stop our talk."

"Why?" the coyote asked.

"Because yonder comes a man."

"I see him," said the coyote, "but he has no gun."

"That's true."

"He has no stick."

"That's true also."

"He has no rock."

"Not in sight."

"Then," went on the coyote, "why should we leave yet? I am afraid of an armed man, but I am not afraid of an unarmed man."

"Well, I am," the crow said. "I have a disconfidence in all men . . . That man we see might have a rock hidden in his pocket. Adios."

And the crow flew over the river.

> *The man the crow in the story saw was a white man. And what he had learned from the white man— and what he shared with the coyote—was that the white man intended to kill him if he could.*
>
> *This is all I have to tell you now. I hope that you will think about it.*
>
> *Respectfully,*
>
> *Joe Hill, Chairman*
> *Tamaya Pueblo*

From her perch in front of the San Ysidro Mini Mart, Natalie watched the afternoon wind lift a blue-and-yellow Wal-Mart bag in a sweeping arc. Never had a Wal-Mart bag looked so lovely, Natalie thought, and yet she was achingly aware that that beauty had never been part of its intention. The apocalypse, she thought, will be marked by thousands of Wal-Mart bags, all whipped by unimpeded winds until they are caught on barbed-wire fences, where they will tatter away into millions of blue plastic shreds.

Next to her, Ralph patiently licked the thick slab of vanilla ice cream wedged between two soft chocolate wafers. There was a method to eating an ice cream sandwich, he'd informed her solemnly. This was Step One.

Natalie tucked an errant strand of hair back into her ponytail and watched the Wal-Mart bag loop toward its destined fence. Once she and Ralph had regained the highway, Natalie had felt her mood darken, and the determinedly cheery yellow smiley face on the bag soured it still more.

Natalie was angry with herself for this mood shift, and yet she was powerless to change it. This should, she thought, be one of the happiest days of her life: Not only had she met her first coyote face-to-face, she'd been present when he'd been set free. She'd watched him run as only a wild creature could, and she'd learned that Ralph Sandoval did something like this nearly every week. It was as if he'd read the Braille of her dreams and could draw what she could only imagine.

Yet now it was over. Yes, she could join Ralph again. But no future time would equal this first one. And, as exhilarating as it had been, this first one had not been what she had imagined. Nothing ever came close to her dreams. In the end, reality was sadly lacking.

Why so blue? Ralph asked. When Natalie looked his way, he held his ice cream sandwich out toward her. She saw that he'd reached Step Two, the first corner.

Natalie smiled and shook her head, then considered Ralph's question. She decided he deserved a response. I think it's because it's over, she said.

Ralph took another bite and chewed thoughtfully. It's never over, he said after he'd swallowed.

Natalie watched the Wal-Mart bag arc skyward in a sudden updraft. You know, she said, I think you're an optimist and I'm a pessimist.

Nah. You're a dreamer and I'm a realist.

His words stopped Natalie as surely as a locked gate. A dreamer? No. Sherman was the dreamer. She was the one who plodded through reality, doing the best she could, one day at a time. It was Sherman who chased after his imagination, who dared to try to create a life that matched it.

But maybe someone who did that was a realist, Natalie thought now. She glanced at Ralph, who had whittled his ice cream sandwich to half its original size. Maybe a dreamer was someone who *preferred* dreams, who'd learned that reality would never come close to them. Which made a realist—

I can see the smoke coming out of your ears, Ralph said.

Natalie smiled. You have a way of making me think in entirely new directions.

Ralph nodded. Yeah. Nina says that, too. It's just how I am, I guess.

Natalie knew what he meant. He wasn't someone who was purposefully contrary, like some of the self-consciously brilliant people with whom she'd gone to college whose carefully inserted bon mots were meant to both showcase their cleverness and make everyone else feel inferior. Ralph was—what was the word?—straightforward, that was it. There was no artifice to Ralph, no attempt to sway or to awe. He was just who he was. And who he was, was someone Natalie liked more and more the better she got to know him.

If she were honest with herself, she realized, she would say that Ralph Sandoval was the kind of man she wished Sherman were. No. Natalie refused to allow herself this thought. She loved her brother just as he was. And he loved her just as she was. Mutual acceptance was what she and Sherman were all about.

An all-too-familiar qualm nibbled at the edge of Natalie's consciousness. Rather than allow it something tasty, she wondered what Sherman was doing now. She wondered if he'd found Alison Lomez. She wondered how Alison Lomez felt about being found. She wondered if she weren't just a little bit jealous of Alison Lomez. Then she stopped herself from going there and watched as the Wal-Mart bag impaled itself on a fence barb and tried in vain to sail free.

After Mommy goes Rachel and Sherman begin to play Candy Land. Sherman gets to go first but then he gets stuck and Rachel goes ahead of him. So long sucker, she says, like someone on TV, and Sherman says, Don't count me out yet, Shirley. My name's not Shirley, Rachel says. And mine's not Sucker, says Sherman. He makes her laugh and laugh.

Rachel doesn't care if Mommy ever comes back. She doesn't care about Daddy either, or Didi, or Molly, or Suzy Charles, or anyone at all. She doesn't even care about Chris her coyote now that Sherman is her friend. She thinks she won't even care if Sherman wins Candy Land but maybe she will care about that, a little.

Now she is stuck. When Sherman passes her, he says *Hasta la vista*, baby. Rachel remembers Daddy saying that, and she remembers what he said next, too, so she says, I'll be back, in a silly voice like a crooked man. Now she has made Sherman laugh and she thinks she is the happiest she has ever been. She hopes this happily ever after will go on and on and she makes herself laugh for a long time after the laughing is already gone. At first Sherman laughs too but then he doesn't anymore, no matter how much Rachel makes the laughing that is not real come out. Then she sees that Sherman is not even looking at Candy Land any more. He is looking out the window toward the mountain.

It is your turn, she tells him, even though it isn't, and Sherman turns back to the game board. So it is, he says. So it is.

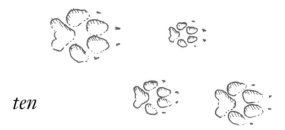

ten

Coyote Facts

Range: Coyotes range from North to South America, throughout Canada, Alaska and even into the Arctic. Coyotes are widespread throughout the United States. Lone coyotes may travel great distances, as much as hundreds of miles.

Alison sprinted toward the main canal, where she could run along the hard-packed dirt next to the irrigation ditch for several miles uninterrupted by other roads. As her legs and breathing settled into their rhythm, Alison let her mind fall into it as well. Free of fear and worry as she hadn't been since Chris had told her about Didi three months before, Alison soon found that the rhythm was all there was: *inhale* left right *exhale* left right *inhale* left right *exhale* left right.

Just as she reached the ditch bank, Alison felt her mind open into clarity, a bright place she could both taste and feel. Though she ran nearly every morning, it had been months since she'd had a runner's high. Elated, she increased her pace. Light poufs of dust accented her footfalls as if the contact her shoes made with the ground were electric. It felt electric. Alison felt electric.

As she passed the adobe yard, she heard a chorus of men holler their approval in Spanish. Alison waved. The men waved back. She pounded north, as if, running, she might reach the Jemez, rising darkly twenty miles to the north. On the other side of the ditch, cars crawled the asphalt at what seemed a much slower pace than hers. Occasionally, someone honked and Alison waved without looking their way.

But she wasn't thinking anything. Not really. This was why she ran, the place she ran toward but seldom arrived. It was as if she had merged with the earth and sky and wind, as if she cut through the air unimpeded, an element, a kindred spirit. Alison could run this way forever, and so she ran and ran and ran. It seemed as if there were nothing between her and the mountains but desire. Perhaps she could get there, if she tried.

Then, suddenly, a coyote dashed across her path. It

didn't slow, even for the irrigation ditch. From Alison's vantage point, it appeared to fly over the water, land nimbly on the other side and dart across the road without slowing.

Alison hadn't slowed either, hadn't had time to register what she'd seen. Now she missed a beat. The bubble of her high burst. She scanned the yards across the road, but the coyote had already disappeared. Alison thought perhaps she'd dreamed it, so quickly had it rushed past.

But she hadn't dreamed it. Now she felt every footfall, her heart thudding in her chest, her breath laboring in her throat. She slowed to a plodding jog that in no way resembled her inspired flight of a moment before. *Thud*, she heard. *Thud, thud, thud.* Alison had fallen back to earth, and with her fall came gravity and its weighty reminders.

To the editor:

It pleases me to see that villagers have begun positing possible solutions to our coyote problem. Chairman Hill's story, for example, provides a solid foundation from which we may be able to begin to successfully build something of value for all Valle Bosqueleños. Many believe that the old myths are far more than mere stories; even scholars now assert that these stories contain lessons that we might do well to heed in our ever-more-fractured times.

I am struck in particular by the concept that if we show the coyote our willingness to share rather than steal, the coyote might do the same. It is known that the only creature that gorges itself beyond sating is the human; it follows that a sated coyote will not need to kill domestic animals.

To this end, I have decided to leave out a bit of hamburger this evening. If this gesture saves one cat's life, then it will have been worth it. What say you, neighbors? Shall we give Chairman Hill's idea a try?

Sincerely,

Sharon Putnam

To the editor:

If I understand Chief Hill and Professor Putnam right, they're saying that if you give a coyote a free lunch, then he won't steal your livestock. I know a lot of people think the Indians know a whole lot more about living here in the desert than the rest of us do, but I got to tell you. I think if I left out a Big Mac for those coyotes, they'd come back the next night wanting two Big Macs, and the night after that wanting four. Let me say where I stand loud and clear: <u>The coyotes are not like us</u>. Sorry, Chief. Sorry, Professor Putnam. Sorry, Ms. Harold. Sorry, coyotes. Call me stubborn, but I just don't see how we can "coexist." And I'll be damned if I'll waste a Big Mac on a coyote.

Jim Curtis

Ralph didn't seem in any hurry to get back in the pickup once he'd finished his ice cream sandwich. With her arm, Natalie shielded her eyes from the bright sun that warmed the storefront, occasionally taking a sip from the bottle of water she'd bought.

It was peaceful here at the San Ysidro Mini Mart, peaceful in a way an asphalt pad between convenience store and highway oughtn't be. The Wal-Mart bag remained skewered on its metal fence post, the only reminder of its flight an occasional ballooning effort when the wind aimed just so.

Times like this, I wish I still smoked, Ralph said. He leaned his plastic chair far back against the stucco wall and propped his feet against the weighty rectangle of a trashcan.

I never smoked, Natalie said, for something to say.

You know who smoked, was that coyote. I never seen one run like he did.

As if he knew where he was going, said Natalie. She felt Ralph glance in her direction before resuming his survey of the parking lot.

Yeah, that's kind of what I was thinking. Doesn't make much sense, though.

Natalie turned her chair so the sun was no longer directly in her eyes but also so she could see Ralph without turning her head. What do you think about the coyotes? she asked him. I mean, I know you've decided to catch-and-release as many as you can. But what do you think?

You mean like about those letters you and Jim Curtis and them write to the paper?

Natalie was careful to keep her face neutral. Yes.

You see that one that Indian wrote? About the crow and the coyote talking in a tree?

I think the crow was in the tree and the coyote on the ground beneath.

Yeah, whatever. I got a good laugh out of that one.

His idea isn't without merit.

You think if people left cheeseburgers out, the coyotes would leave their roosters alone?

Natalie felt her face color. Now you're laughing at me.

Do I look like I'm laughing? I'm asking you, what do you think?

Didn't I ask you first?

You did, said Ralph. And I told you what I thought.

You asked me about Joe Hill's letter. You didn't tell me what you thought.

Joe Hill—oh. The Indian. Well, I thought he was having a good laugh himself, but he was trying to say something, too.

And do you think what he was trying to say was worth hearing?

Ralph kicked his seat level and then leaned forward. Natalie leaned forward, too, his shift in position a signal that what he said next would matter. I think whenever anyone tries to say something it's worth hearing, Ralph said. I think half the problems in this world are because people are too busy trying to say things to listen to what other people are trying to say. No, I think ninety percent of the problems in this world are because of that.

Do you think I'm part of the problem?

Ralph looked off toward the forlorn Wal-Mart bag then turned back to her. You want the truth?

I want the truth of what you think.

Ralph opened his hands onto his knees, a gesture a therapist might have noted as *nothing to hide*, Natalie thought. I think sometimes you don't hear what other people are saying when it don't fit in with what you're trying to say, Ralph said. Or you'll turn a thing someone else says so it does fit. He held his hand up, as if to stop her speaking, though she hadn't been about to. But here's the thing: I think everybody does that. How do we get by in this world, if we don't have a picture we try to fit everything into? When things don't fit into our picture, we don't have many choices. We can ignore them like they're not even there, or we can decide to change the picture we got.

Natalie smiled. You're quite the philosopher, she said.

Ralph shrugged his shoulders. I spend a lot of time alone in my truck is all.

You weren't always like this?

Another shrug. Shit if I know.

I can see why Nina married you.

Ralph barked out a laugh. Oh, you can, can you? That's something I've wondered about some myself.

Natalie looked at Ralph. He was methodically licking the wrapper of his ice cream sandwich clean. How unaffected he was. How unconcerned for what others might think. It was as if no one had ever told him that it was what others thought that mattered in the end. All at once, Natalie had to know his secret.

Ralph, she said. Ralph looked up from the wrapper and tilted his head, waiting for what she would ask him.

Ralph, she said again. She couldn't think how to phrase what she wanted to say.

I'm all ears, said Ralph, pulling on one for emphasis.

At his urging, Natalie plunged. How can you be yourself? she asked. I mean, how do you do what you do without worrying what others think?

Ralph tilted his head again, considering her question. Why would I worry about what someone else was thinking? he said at last. What's that got to do with what I do?

Natalie pressed on. But what's the secret to being that way? How do you not care?

Ralph shook his head. Oh, it's not that I don't care, he said. I guess maybe it's that I trust myself a whole lot more than any old person thinks they know better than me. It's funny, how some people think they know so much, they think they can tell other people how to do things they don't know shit about. I always listen to 'em, though. Sometimes I even learn something. But in the end, I figure, you got to trust your own gut, not someone else's, you know what I mean?

Natalie nodded slowly. I do and I don't, she said. I mean I do trust my own gut, as you phrase it. But whenever someone else questions me, and as you know, she smiled, that happens fairly regularly in the *Valle Bosque Beacon*, that same gut sends off a flutter of alarms, a sort of internal warning that says, You might be wrong. Stop. Look. Listen.

Ralph laughed. Oh, Ms. Harold, he said. That ain't what that feeling is saying. It's like when you think you hear a mouse in the wall. It makes you feel funny inside, knowing it, but it ain't saying you're wrong.

Natalie, she said, with sudden conviction. Call me Natalie.

Ralph shook his head. Natalie, he said.

She liked the way he said her name. She smiled again. He made it sound like it mattered. What is that feeling saying then?

You really think I know the answer? Ralph asked. Natalie nodded. Okay, then. Ralph looked off toward the highway, as if the answer might be rising genie-like from the asphalt. Then he turned back toward her. I think it's saying that what you're doing is taking a chance, he said. I think it's saying that you might not succeed at whatever you're trying to do. And I think it's saying that you have a choice: You can go ahead and take that chance, even though you don't know what will happen if you do; or you can play it safe and never know what might have been.

Natalie could feel that fluttering feeling now. Like when you think you hear a mouse in the wall, Ralph had said. And what have you discovered, when you've taken those chances? she asked.

Ralph laughed again. You know what? Most of the time it turns out I wasn't taking a chance after all. Most of the time the only thing that was really stopping me was myself. You know what I mean?

I do, Natalie said. She turned to watch the Wal-Mart bag again, only to discover that it wasn't where she'd last seen it. Somehow, it had torn free of the fencepost and was once again soaring jauntily on another gust of wind.

Ain't that something? Ralph said. Never thought I'd wish I was a Wal-Mart bag.

Natalie couldn't help it. She laughed. What had happened to her grey mood? Ralph had erased it as surely as if she'd been a blackboard, easily wiped clean. How could you be thinking precisely what I am? she asked him. Are you a mind-reader? A psychic? A man who sees through walls?

Nah, said Ralph. But who wouldn't want to be that bag, just flying on a breeze?

But not everyone would notice it.

Maybe not, Ralph conceded. Their loss, huh?

Natalie finished the water in her bottle and tossed it toward the center of the concrete trash bin. It went in. For someone who'd always been picked last or not at all during gym classes, this was close to miraculous, and for a brief moment Natalie thought she understood what made successful athletes gloat.

You want another bottle? Ralph asked. I'm gonna get a Pepsi for the road.

Yes, thank you, said Natalie.

Could she be someone who took chances? she wondered. Someone who didn't worry about what others thought? Through the store window, she watched Ralph say something to the Pueblo woman behind the counter. The woman laughed. How would Ralph answer these questions? she wondered. At once, she answered: He'd say they were mutually exclusive. You could be someone who took chances who still worried what others thought, or you could be someone who never risked a thing but didn't give a hoot about others, either.

But I can't separate them, Natalie answered the Ralph in her mind. If I take a chance, others may see me for the fool that I am.

You take chances every day, the imaginary Ralph answered. Every time you write one of them letters. And even though Jim Curtis and others like him attack you, you keep on doing it.

Yes, Natalie thought. I do. But that doesn't feel like a risk to me. Not anymore. Why is that?

We forget that the things we do every day can matter,

said the Ralph in her head, because they're the things we do every day.

Natalie was pleased not only to have discovered this truth, but to have emulated Ralph's thinking so well. Now the real Ralph came out of the store, still laughing. You ready? he asked.

Natalie rose in reply, noting as she did that the Wal-Mart bag was once again ensnared on a fence barb. Now that she'd made Ralph's mind her own, she could say anything to the Ralph that stood before her. I know what that feels like, she said with a nod toward the bag on the fence.

Don't we all, said Ralph. Don't we all.

Alison stretched toward the foot she'd propped on the trunk of a cottonwood. Now that she'd stopped running, she'd become aware of the insistent spring wind and was anxious to start toward home, but knew better than to rush through her cool-downs. As a loud muffler declared a dirt bike racing by on the other side of the ditch, Alison unfolded to a stand and began her uphill jog.

In her mind, she kept seeing the coyote run across her path. The ghost coyote, she had already named it, as if she couldn't be entirely certain it had existed. She wondered if it were the same coyote, the one Rachel called Chris. She wondered where it was coming from and where it was going, though she thought she knew the latter: It had been pointed in the direction she jogged now, toward her home.

Along with the prickle of the coyote's threat, though, Alison nonetheless found herself exhilarated by the way it had run. Maybe it was because she was a runner herself.

Maybe she understood the desire to run that way, the way running could make you feel. When Alison was running, she forgot about Rachel. She forgot about Chris and about Didi, about work and Molly and coyotes and what to make for dinner. When Alison was running, the world receded to a pinpoint far behind her.

Which was why, when Alison headed back after a run, the pinpoint would swell larger and larger, taking on mass and shape until everything she'd left behind while she'd been running assumed gigantic proportions. Today the theme seemed to be what ifs. What if the coyote were running toward her house? What if Rachel weren't better and Alison came back to find her feverish, or worse? What if Sherman were after all not what he seemed, and so—and here Alison hesitated before forcing herself to finish the question—what if she'd left her daughter with someone she shouldn't have? Yes, she'd considered this before she'd left, and dismissed her worries as foolishness. Now, though, her worst fears tumbled forth. What if, even now, Sherman were harming Rachel in some way Alison couldn't begin to imagine but would regret forever after? What if— Alison couldn't go any further. Instead, she increased her pace, blowing out in short huffs as she ran.

The road sloped upward all the way to the Mesa Playa subdivision, a gradual incline, true, but uphill all the same. Alison's house was tucked into its cul-de-sac in such a way that she couldn't see it until she was nearly there. Not that its exterior would reveal a thing. Alison would need to burst in without warning to catch Sherman in the act. In the act of what? Alison wasn't sure, and the uncertainty upped her pace still more.

In her haste, she turned her corner more sharply than she intended and came down hard on her left ankle. She felt at once the spike of pain that spelled a sprain and swore aloud. But she didn't slow. She eked her key from its Velcro slot in her jacket and stopped only long enough to unlock the back door before bursting into the kitchen, then rushed on to the living room without closing the door behind her.

Sherman and Rachel looked up from their game board and then back without so much as a hello. Alison stood there, gradually becoming aware of how she must look—red-faced, sweating, panting—and of how her ankle had begun to throb. Then she limped back into the kitchen.

After closing the back door, Alison leaned against the wall to catch her breath and maybe, the way she'd felt before she'd left for her run, when a change to her life had seemed possible. Both were elusive. What insisted itself instead was the tenderness in her ankle and her own foolishness, for leaving Rachel here in the first place, and for worrying about her once she had. A bead of sweat dropped to her spandex tights, bringing her back to where she was, and she hobbled to a kitchen chair and sat down to gingerly remove the offending shoe and sock.

Sherman came in as she was rolling up her pant leg to examine the ankle more closely. Ice, he said, pointing toward the swelling but not touching it. Without waiting for her to respond, he filled a Baggie with ice, then wrapped it in a dishtowel and set it on her propped ankle. He followed up with a glass of water, which Alison gulped gratefully.

She'd been wrong about him, of course, just as she was wrong about everything. She thought too much and acted too little, second-guessed when she should have gotten it right the first time, and then third-guessed when the second guess went awry. She was a damned fool to boot, and what this man was doing here, not just helping her but smiling at her as well, was beyond her ken. She wanted to tell him to get out while he could, that Alison was someone with whom he wouldn't want to become entangled. Then she realized that she'd yet to say a word since she'd stormed through the door.

Thanks, she said.

You're welcome.

Rachel bounced into the kitchen, crossing her arms in miniature imitation of Alison herself. What did you do? she asked, another echo.

Who won? Alison asked her instead.

Rachel looked over at Sherman and smiled. I let Sherman win, she said.

I won fair and square, he retorted.

Alison sighed, and both turned to her. Does it hurt? Sherman asked.

I don't know. It's frozen.

He held out an arm. You should get more comfortable. Lie down on the couch.

I stink. I need a shower.

A bath might be better. So you don't have to stand. I'll even draw it for you.

Did people still *draw* baths? Alison wondered. Apparently Sherman did. Before she could either thank him or protest, he was off. A bath would be heavenly, she thought. A bath in the middle of the afternoon: What an odd day this was turning into. No. What an odd day it had already been.

I'm hungry, Rachel said. Alison had forgotten she was standing there. When she looked, she saw that Rachel's arms were still crossed over her chest.

Can you get yourself some string cheese from the fridge? Alison asked her. If you bring it here, I'll peel it for you.

Rachel didn't move. Did you really hurt your leg or are you just pretending?

Alison felt herself jerk in surprise. Where had that come from? Why would I pretend? she asked, doing her best to keep her tone neutral.

Well, I don't *know*, said Rachel. Then she marched to the fridge and extracted two sticks of string cheese before disappearing back into the living room. A moment later, Alison heard the TV click on, and then the theme from *Blue's Clues*. Everything's fine, she told herself, but her ankle throbbed a rebuttal.

It is fun playing Candy Land with Sherman. He doesn't read a book in between like Mommy or forget how to play like Daddy. He doesn't cheat like Suzy Charles or get mad like Suzy does sometimes, too. What Rachel likes best about Sherman is how he doesn't even try to make her like him. He is just who he is. He is not pretending, or acting different from how he feels, or saying he is not mad when he is really absolutely furious.

When Mommy comes back she looks mad like she gets at Daddy so Rachel pretends like she isn't even there until Mommy goes to the kitchen. But then Sherman says, Do you think your Mom's okay? and Rachel feels like she should tell him the truth because he is her friend, so she says, I don't know. She wants to tell him that it is hard to know what Mommy feels, because how she feels and what she says are two different things, but she doesn't say that because she is not sure of the right words to tell how she knows it is.

I'll just check on her, Sherman says, and then he goes in the kitchen, too. Rachel knows then it is Mommy Sherman likes best, not her, and then she hates Mommy so much she hopes she is dead. But then she remembers that thinking it can make it happen, and she gets scared that she has killed Mommy, so she goes to the kitchen to see.

When Rachel gets there, though, there is Mommy with her puffy ankle. Sherman is putting ice on it and Mommy looks like someone Rachel doesn't even know, which is the scariest thing of all. Rachel feels like crying like a baby but she doesn't. She knows what she has to do now. She will be the Mommy. She will make everything all right.

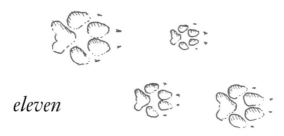

eleven

> No other animal has stirred up more human emotion
> than the coyote does by simply being the coyote—a
> medium-sized predator with forty-two teeth, trying to
> eat, raise some young, and keep alive.

Eagle, said Ralph. Without slowing the pickup, he leaned across the dashboard and pointed toward a solitary dead piñon tree atop a ridge.

Natalie twisted in the direction he pointed as they sped past and was rewarded with a glimpse of the biggest bird she had ever seen. It loomed above the tree, an exclamation point. Is it a bald eagle? she asked as she turned to faced forward again.

Yeah. Goldens are smaller, closer to hawks. Lots of balds around these days. They've come back.

It occurred to Natalie that, like the coyote, the bald eagle was a predator. Then it occurred to her that one was revered, the other reviled. It's interesting the government would protect a predator, she said to Ralph.

Ralph shook his head. You're thinking that even though they do the same thing as a coyote, killing livestock and such, they got a different reputation.

Natalie smiled. Mind-reading again, she said. But yes, that is what I was thinking. Why do you suppose one ends up our national emblem and the other our public enemy?

Ralph considered. He steered the pickup with his left hand, his right resting lightly on the gear shift knob. Natalie watched him tap a rhythm with his fingers while he thought. That's a good question, he said after a while. Way I see it is people figure anything can just spread its wings and fly matters a whole lot more than something needs four legs to walk instead of two. We look up at an eagle. We look down on a coyote.

Literally or figuratively?

Ralph shook his head again. Natalie had come to realize it wasn't the negative gesture it appeared, but rather agreement with what she *hadn't* said. Both, he answered.

Now it was Natalie's turn to consider. If what Ralph said were true, the coyote would always be looked down upon, no matter how much people like her tried to raise others' awareness. But Natalie had spent enough time in the company of therapists to learn some things about human nature. One of the things one had liked to point out was that the need to feel in control, and hence superior, was intrinsic, and that to stand taller than something or someone else was to be its master. People looked down on whomever and whatever they could.

When it came to things that other creatures did easily that weren't humanly possibly, however, people took a different tack. People couldn't fly, for example, so they admired creatures like birds that could. It followed that admiration for the largest bird most had ever seen made that bird naturally emblematic of all that humans hoped they might be. Never mind what an eagle ate. When it soared through the sky, anything was possible. Natalie outlined her ruminations for Ralph.

Ralph shook his head in agreement. Did you know that most U.S. Presidents have been over six feet tall? he asked her.

I won't ask how that connects to the present conversation.

It does, though. If you were to put two people next to each other, one tall and one short, and ask which one would make a better leader, almost everyone would pick the tall one, the one they figure they can look up to.

It was Natalie's turn to shake her head. It's awfully simplistic, she said.

So are people, Ralph said as if it were a closing argument. Maybe it was. They settled back into companionable silence, the miles unfurling beneath them. Natalie thought about Ralph's eye for natural detail, how he'd spotted the eagle in the first place. Natalie always looked straight ahead, carefully watching to see where she was going because she didn't like surprises, but because of this tendency, the eagle hadn't been in her visual field.

But it had been in Ralph's. That suggested that Ralph

embraced a much bigger picture than her more focused vision. Natalie didn't like what this said about her.

But wasn't it true? Even Sherman sometimes accused her of having tunnel vision. You might as well be wearing blinders, he'd said to her once. What had they been talking about?

Of course. They'd been talking, as they so often seemed to, about Sherman. And Natalie had been defending him against his far more jaded—and perhaps more realistic—own view of himself.

This had been just after he'd departed L.A. He'd left behind a mess that included unpaid rent, an angry ex-girlfriend owed money, even, if Natalie remembered correctly, something about a racehorse he'd convinced someone else to buy that had come up lame. Natalie had written checks from her trust account to quiet it all. He'll never learn if you keep doing that, the ex-girlfriend had said, but she had accepted the money. When she had called to thank Natalie, she said Sherman was all cover and no book.

You don't deserve someone like Sherman, Natalie told her. She could feel her grip on the receiver tighten as she said it.

No one deserves someone like Sherman, the ex-girlfriend retorted. Then she slammed down the phone without saying goodbye.

When Natalie related this exchange to Sherman, she highlighted the girlfriend's immaturity, how she couldn't even complete a conversation in the appropriate manner. You're well rid of that one, she told him. As it was January, they were having their customary martinis in the living room rather than outside. Because Natalie hated the long grey of winter, the lamps were illuminated all day, even when, as now, the sun hadn't yet set.

Face it, Nat, Sherman replied. I'm no prize. In fact, I'm doing my best to coast along. The fewer bumps along the way, the better.

Natalie examined her brother's features in the lamplight, noting a surprising sharpness that on someone else she might have read as deception. Not on Sherman, of course. He must just be tired, she told herself before responding. There's nothing wrong with that, she said.

When Sherman shook his head, the shadows arched his eyebrows. You wouldn't say that if it weren't me doing it.

You sell yourself short, Natalie insisted. She'd stopped looking at his face.

Sherman laughed, then held out his martini glass for a refill. He watched as she poured, then raised his glass to her. You sell me long, he said, then took a sip. You always did. You might as well be wearing blinders when it comes to me.

I shouldn't think you would complain of it, Natalie said. She turned the stem of her martini glass in her hands, watched the way it caught the light and sent it dancing.

You're right. I should be grateful. I *am* grateful. Sherman lifted his glass to her again. Thank you, my champion. I salute you.

Natalie caught the sarcasm in his voice and felt her face color. She took a sip of her martini so Sherman wouldn't notice. Then she realized that it wasn't likely Sherman *would* notice, because her blushing wasn't about him. Sherman wasn't selfish, but he *was* self-focused. He deserved to be that way, Natalie insisted to herself.

But because of what he'd just said, her blinders were momentarily off and Natalie felt the barb of a Sherman she preferred to pretend didn't exist. She didn't like him. She willed him gone.

Let me make dinner, Sherman said then, as if he'd heard her thoughts. Natalie nodded her assent.

After he'd left her alone in the living room, she reminded herself that a selfish person wouldn't offer to make dinner after driving fifteen hours without a break. And there were other things Sherman had done over the years that showed how much he cared. She reminded herself how he had applauded her decisions to leave Vassar, to abandon poetry, to learn more about coyotes. No one supported her as unambiguously as Sherman did. And she did the same for him.

Ralph braked the pickup sharply. Natalie lurched forward into her shoulder strap. Sorry about that, Ralph said, pointing into the sage to their right. See 'im?

Natalie looked but didn't see.

Black bear. Probably just woke up.

Natalie was at once heartsick. She'd missed seeing a black bear. She'd miss everything if she didn't learn to pay closer attention. She resolved to make certain she didn't miss another thing. How do you do that? she asked Ralph. Spot things off the road?

Actually, that fella was *in* the road. Good thing I *did* spot him, or he'd be a mashed bear.

So now she was missing what was right in front of her. It was worse than blinders; it was blindness itself. Natalie shunted Sherman from her mind and focused on the highway. But no matter how hard she tried, all she could see was the swath of black it cut as it climbed the last mesa before they descended once more into the valley.

To the editor:

Mr. Curtis has succeeded in making me laugh. Big Macs, indeed. The hamburger I left out was missing when I checked in the morning, but as it didn't happen in front of me, there is no way for me to know if the diner was coyote, hawk, or neighborhood mongrel. It occurred to me, however, that if it were a bird or dog, I would not feel the same about its disappearance. It seems we reserve our awe—and our revulsion—for the coyote. Why is this, do you suppose? I would posit that the answer to this question might also provide the beginning of an answer to our more pressing one: how we might learn to live with our coyote neighbors without gunning them down.

Sincerely,

Sharon Putnam

To the editor:

A friend suggested that we revere the eagle because it flies above us, while we look down on the coyote because it walks beneath us. I hope all Valle Bosqueleños will consider this equation the next time they revile a coyote.

Sincerely,

Natalie Harold

To the editor:

Hey, welcome back, Ms. Harold. I actually missed hearing what you had to say about your friends the coyotes. You bet I look down on them. So here's an equation for you: coyote + gun = dead coyote.

Jim Curtis

Alison eased herself into the warm water, carefully elevated her ankle on the rim of the tub, then lay her head back and closed her eyes. Again and again, the coyote darted across her path, soared over the irrigation ditch, and disappeared toward Mesa Playa, and every time it disappeared, Alison tasted the now-familiar copper of fear.

What was she afraid of? It wasn't the coyote, not exactly. What she was afraid of, Alison thought, was the unexpected: the glitch in the works, the bolt from the blue, the sudden microburst of wind. That was how it had been the night Chris had come home and told her about Didi, and even now, three months later, Alison was still wary. It must be the way war veterans felt, though she could hardly compare her relatively easy life to theirs. And yet, she did feel shell-shocked. Or at any rate thought she understood the origin of the phrase.

Alison opened her eyes to set a loofah under her throbbing ankle, then settled back again. Chris had gotten home before her that night, so her routine had already been upset before she walked through the door. You're home early, she said when she saw him sitting at the kitchen counter.

I wanted to talk to you, he said.

Where's Rachel? Alison asked. She leaned on the counter, but she didn't sit down.

I sent her next door to play with Suzy Charles. Chris took a sip from a bottle of Corona he'd already half finished.

Alison found herself reading the label. *La Cerveza Mas Fina*. The beer most fine. I don't like Suzy Charles, she said. She puts ideas in Rachel's head.

Don't change the subject, Alison. I need to talk to you.

Something about the way he said it made Alison suddenly dizzy. She swayed, then grabbed a stool and sat. What? she asked.

I met someone, said Chris.

Good for you, Alison said before she could stop herself.

Chris stood so suddenly a splash of beer sloshed out of his bottle onto the countertop. Well, that was easy, he said, adopting the same sarcastic tone as she. *Sayonara*. But he didn't leave.

Alison watched the beer puddle slowly spread. She reached across and touched it with the tip of her index finger, then put the finger in her mouth. I need a drink, she said.

Help yourself, said Chris.

Alison didn't move. After watching her for a moment, Chris opened the fridge, poured her a glass of Merlot, and set it in front of her. Alison nodded her thanks, then took a long sip.

Who is it? she asked.

No one you know. Her name's Didi.

A patient?

Chris shook his head. Jack Zamora introduced us.

Thanks, Jack. Alison took another sip of wine.

Alison, I wasn't looking to fall in love. It just happened.

Alison figured that was true, but she wasn't going to give, not an inch. She might be better off without Chris, she knew. Already in the brief seconds since he'd told her, she'd begun visualize a life without him. She pictured herself and Rachel coming home to a house stripped of its battles— Rachel, she thought. What about Rachel? she said. Are you going to tell her or are you going to leave that to me?

Chris hung his head. I'll tell her. Then he looked across the island at Alison. It isn't as if we were *happy*, Alison. We've never been happy. You know that.

We were okay, though. Sometimes we were okay. Even as she said it, Alison knew it wasn't so.

Most of the time we weren't okay. There's plenty of times I could have killed you.

I could kill you right now, she said. How's that?

Chris laughed. You don't know which end of a gun is up.

I could stab you. I could slip rat poison into your beer. I could trip you so you hit your head on the countertop. Down you'd go. Your little love bunny would be so disappointed.

Her name's Didi.

What kind of name is Didi, for chrissake?

Deirdre. It's short for Deirdre.

Deirdre, Alison said in a nasal voice not her own.

Stop it, Alison. Don't piss me off. You're just making it harder for both of us.

I don't imagine it's all that hard on you.

Chris's fist came down hard on the countertop. You

don't know shit, Alison. You think you do, but you don't.

And you do? Alison said far more calmly than she felt. She finished her wine with a casual lift of the glass, as if her husband left her every day. This could be the best thing that ever happened to you, she told herself. But she didn't believe it. Not then. Not yet.

You okay? The voice came from the other side of the bathroom door. Alison's eyes flew open. Sherman.

I'm fine, she said. She turned on the hot water with her right big toe. Do you need me to rescue you from Rachel?

Just wanted to make sure you hadn't drowned, Sherman said. How's your ankle?

Alison lobbed it experimentally. Better, I think. I'll be out soon.

Take your time, Sherman said. We're watching *Sesame Street*. The things one can learn from daytime television.

Alison twisted the tap off with the same toe. Carry on, she said.

Sherman was so unlike Chris that Alison could find no basis on which to compare them. She tried to imagine Chris in the situation Sherman was in now, but she couldn't get him there. Then she tried to imagine Sherman into the night Chris had told her about Didi, but he refused to morph. Next, she tried to imagine Sherman saying any of the things Chris had routinely said to her, herself saying to Sherman the things she'd routinely said to Chris. No. This time was different. She wouldn't make the same mistakes she'd made with Chris. She wouldn't let her wicked tongue drive Sherman off. In fact, she vowed, she'd make certain Sherman never even made its acquaintance.

When Sherman comes back he says, What'd I miss? Rachel doesn't answer him. On the television, the number 5 is making a star. One-two-three-four-*five*! the points of the star sing, one at a time. Five-four-three-two-*one*! Every point of the star lights up a different color when they sing. Rachel already knows what comes next, because she has watched this one before, so she sings with the colors when they light up. Red-blue-green-yellow-*orange*! Red-blue-green-yellow-*orange*! The third time, Sherman sings, too, and he gets it just right. Red-blue-green-yellow-*orange*! Even after the singing star is gone and Oscar comes out of his garbage can Rachel and Sherman keep singing red-blue-green-yellow-*orange*! over and over again. Rachel and Sherman laugh and laugh and sing and sing and Rachel thinks that Daddy never sang with her this way or Mommy either and that maybe she will go live with Sherman. She thinks he must live in a castle like a handsome prince. *Someday my prince will come*, Snow White sang, and now Rachel knows why she was singing. And now she knows the difference between someday and forever, too. Someday is a place you can get to. Forever is a place where you already are.

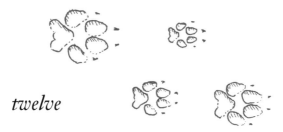

twelve

Although humans and coyotes have shared the same environment for centuries, most observations of coyotes have been made over the sights of rifles.

Natalie asked Ralph to drop her off along the ditch bank a few miles from her home so she could reflect on the day's events while walking. Not only was she not yet ready to be inside, there was also the question of whether she would find Sherman at home when she got there, or if, as she suspected, he had gone off in search of Alison Lomez. She didn't want to know the answer to this question yet, either.

Natalie was accustomed to solitude, so, while she had found Ralph Sandoval an all-in-all agreeable companion, the long period spent with another person had left her, finally, edgy and taut. If she walked for a little while, she thought, she could settle back into herself. Besides, it was possible she'd see another coyote in her sojourn. It wasn't merely an empty desire anymore, but something that could happen, that had happened, that could happen again.

After Ralph pulled away, Natalie stood, waiting for the dust the pickup had raised to settle onto the path. On the other side of the canal, a red-blinking school bus discharged screaming grade schoolers onto the road shoulder. Natalie watched the children disappear into waiting Jeeps and Explorers. There was even a maroon Hummer, an obscenity of a vehicle if there ever was one, that swallowed two children without a trace. The school bus doors brayed shut and the bus resumed its southward crawl. Natalie realized it must be close to 4 p.m.

Once the bus and its retinue had dispersed, Natalie had the ditch bank to herself. Ordinarily when she walked in the afternoon, she'd meet dogs and their owners, pairs of horses trotting smartly, the occasional miniature horse pulling a specially made cart, even llamas and goats following their masters placidly on long leather leads. Today's isolation was both unusual and welcome, and Natalie allowed herself to breathe it in deeply before setting out in the direction of her house.

A hundred yards into her walk, she encountered two girls (she guessed them to be about twelve) riding grey ponies side by side. The girls leaned from their saddles toward each other as if naturally drawn and were so caught up in their giggling discussion that they barely acknowledged Natalie as she moved to the side of the path to let them pass.

Next, Natalie met a woman walking three dogs of no particular breed, one black, short-legged, and barrel-chested; another small, grey, and wiry; the third tall and spotted. Each was linked to the woman by a retractable leash that whirred its comings and goings. The woman nodded a greeting and Natalie nodded back. The dogs followed their noses through the growth along the ditch bank and paid her no mind, but Natalie nonetheless felt the taste of her unaccountable fear of dogs rise in her throat.

Soon after, a three-wheeled dirt bike came careening along the dirt path that paralleled the other side of the canal. Natalie knew this was illegal—especially at this speed—but she also knew that many parents found the vehicles convenient babysitters. As the bike flew past, she noted which way the breeze would carry its accompanying dust cloud, then hurried to be out of its way. The roar of the bike lambasted her ears, and then her teeth, and Natalie closed her eyes, as if that would silence the assault. When the sound at last receded, she opened her eyes. The brown dirt had settled, and she was once again alone.

Natalie crossed the final feeder road before her own and began the last mile of uninterrupted path. A few cars meandered along the paved road on the other side of the ditch. When she came to a recent animal dropping, Natalie found a long stick, poked at the scat, and determined that it was coyote. Feeling none of the elation at her discovery she might have before today's adventure, she walked on, keeping the stick, which was a good length for walking. Finding scat used to thrill her, she thought. Now nothing but another coyote would do.

And then one was there. One moment she'd been

alone. The next she most assuredly was not. The coyote that suddenly materialized before her carried something in its mouth, something perhaps still alive, or so recently killed as to appear still alive. The coyote paused in its trot toward her, a mere five feet away. Natalie shrieked, a comical and startling sound. Then she and the coyote stood. Studying each other. Sizing each other up. Weighing their options. Their fears. Their desires.

Natalie found herself focusing on the furred thing that dangled from the coyote's mouth. Black and limp, it was the size of a large cat or a small dog. Or, Natalie reminded herself with effort, a rabbit. It could be a newborn lamb, she thought. A skunk. A squirrel. It could be one of any number of animals, either wild or domestic.

Natalie stood frozen, her eyes riveted, her mind cataloging nonsense as if it mattered. Maybe it did. The coyote stood, too. Looking at her.

Then, low and long, the coyote growled. Natalie felt her heart trip into her throat, where it stuttered like a thing gone wild. She'd forgotten how to breathe. She felt the blood rush from her head. She was going to faint. She couldn't faint. She met the coyote's eyes. It growled again.

The stick. Natalie swept it toward the coyote, and, just like that, the coyote rushed past her, the black thing swinging from its maw as if she had struck it into motion. Natalie whirled to watch the coyote retreat, but it had disappeared into the still-brown weeds that lined the path as if it had never been there at all.

Still panting, Natalie put her hand to her throat. She could feel her heart there, pattering madly. Her fear was something she could taste, the knowledge that the coyote might have hurt her a certainty. In that moment, Natalie understood not just Alison Lomez's concern for her daughter, but Jim Curtis's desire to shoot every coyote he saw. It was fear, she realized, not bravado. But in the next moment, she told herself that this didn't make it right.

As her heartbeat slowed, Natalie forced herself to take one tentative step and then a second, found that she was still able to put one foot in front of the other. Her hand remained at her throat, gauging her heartbeat, and Natalie walked to its rhythm, far faster than she ordinarily did. Periodically, she looked over her shoulder for the coyote, but it was gone.

Natalie was both relieved and disappointed. Now that her encounter was over, she wished it had lasted longer. Already she was translating her fear into something else: surprise, perhaps, or confusion. In her head, she began composing the letter she'd write to the editor of the *Valle Bosque Beacon*, the letter that detailed her own coyote encounter, how one long stick had been enough to chase the coyote away.

But Natalie's mind returned to the thing dangling from the coyote's mouth. She didn't want to go there, and yet she couldn't help it. Was there blood? Natalie didn't think so. She tried to picture the thing as a living creature, to will it into a recognizable shape. The long tail likely spelled cat, though it could have been a squirrel or a skunk. Not a rabbit, then. That made her think about ears, but she didn't recall seeing them. When she tried to focus on what she *had* seen, though, her memory instead provided gore that hadn't been there and Natalie saw internal organs, bloody and exposed.

Without warning, Natalie retched. She dashed to the side of the ditch road and heaved into the dirt. An older man in a well-worn hat walking a Scottie dog stopped and asked her if she were all right and Natalie nodded that she was. Are you sure? the man said. The Scottie sniffed toward her leavings, and the man pulled the leash taut. When Natalie said she was sure, the man walked on, the Scottie pulled reluctantly behind him. The man cast glances over his shoulder until he disappeared around a bend.

Natalie pulled a tissue from her pocket and patted her mouth, then drank the rest of the water from the bottle Ralph had bought her at the San Ysidro Mini Mart. What a long time ago that seemed, she thought. Time was such a fluid thing, collapsing and expanding as if it were a universe with its own set of rules. She thought about Sherman's arrival, just last night. That too seemed to have happened in a distant past.

Still thinking about the nature of time, Natalie began walking again. She thought how recent her childhood sometimes seemed, and was at once walking along Sixth Avenue instead of the ditch bank. Lost in her reverie, Natalie saw herself safely home.

At first, Alison shifted her weight onto the ankle cautiously. Then she put her full weight on her left foot. She could still feel a tenderness, but she wouldn't need to limp, just walk slowly and carefully for a few days. That and not run, she thought. Or run slowly and carefully. She'd see how it felt in the morning before she abandoned her routine entirely, she decided.

Refreshed from her bath, Alison studied the clothes hanging in her closet. She wanted to wear something that Sherman would notice, but she didn't want him to notice that she'd done so. Jeans would work, she thought. She slipped on a favorite pair, then decided on a simple white sweater. She added a turquoise choker Chris had gotten her for her thirtieth birthday. She pulled her hair back from her face experimentally, then decided to leave it be. A little blush, a little lip gloss, one final pat to her hair.

Barefoot, Alison returned to the living room. She found Sherman and Rachel sitting on the couch. On the television, Peter Jennings solemnly recited the latest war news. And, in his usual chair, sat Chris. He gave Alison a scowl so weighted with malice that she felt compelled to lower her eyes before forcing herself to meet his scorn.

What are you *doing* here? she asked.

I brought over the shotgun, like I said I would.

I told you *not* to bring over the shotgun.

Who died and made you queen?

Alison felt Sherman and Rachel watching the exchange. Maybe we should discuss this in the kitchen, she said.

Maybe we should discuss this in the kitchen, Chris repeated, trying (and failing, Alison thought) to mimic her voice.

On the couch, Rachel giggled. Alison shot her a look, but met Sherman's eyes instead. He inclined his head toward the front door, a question: Should I go?

No, Alison mouthed back, then patted the air with her hand, a staying motion. We'll be right back, she said aloud. She felt like an actor in a poorly scripted play.

Chris followed her into the kitchen. Who's the guy? he said before they'd even stopped.

He's a friend, said Alison.

So your *friend* watches TV with my kid while you take a bath?

Rachel's home sick.

She doesn't look sick to me.

She's better.

Chris took a step toward her. Alison took a step back. What's going on here, Alison?

This is *my* house.

And Rachel is *my* kid.

But I'm not *your* wife anymore. Not really. Stop acting like I *am*.

I don't give a shit about you. It's Rachel I'm worried about. Who the fuck *is* this guy, Alison? He answers the door, and when I say I'm Rachel's father, he just lets me in. Lets me *right in*, Alison. I could have been anyone, for chrissake.

But you *are* Rachel's father. Sherman probably knew that.

How would he know that?

You told him you were. You— Alison stopped. She took a breath, let it out. Stop, she said to Chris, holding out her hand like a cop. Let's both just *stop*. Count to ten. Start over. She closed her eyes and began counting.

I don't like it, she heard Chris say.

Five. Six. Seven, said Alison. She kept her eyes closed.

Something's fishy.

Eight. Nine. Ten. Alison opened her eyes. Nothing's fishy. Now tell me why you're really here.

I told you. To drop off the shotgun. It's out in my pickup.

Please don't, Chris. I won't use it, and I'll worry about it being here, with Rachel.

But it's to protect Rache— Chris looked up as Sherman came into the room.

Sherman smiled at Alison. I'd better get going, he said. Natalie's expecting me for dinner.

Who's Natalie? Chris said to Alison as if Sherman weren't there.

His sister, Alison answered. She turned to Sherman. Thanks, she said, though she wanted to say much more. For everything.

I'll call you, he said. He turned to Chris. Good meeting you.

Yeah, said Chris. Alison was glad he didn't say anything more.

I'll walk you to the door, she said to Sherman.

That's okay, Sherman said, a little too quickly, Alison thought. She could feel everything they'd begun to build in the afternoon evaporating, as if it had been made of air. Maybe it had. I'll call you, Sherman repeated. Then he was gone. Alison heard him exchange goodbyes with Rachel, the front door open and close. A moment later, a car started in the drive and then crunched off the gravel and away.

Rachel came to the archway that led to the kitchen but didn't cross the threshold. Sherman left, she said, an accusation.

I know, Swee'pea, said Alison.

Wanna go to McDonald's? Chris asked her.

She may *not* go to McDonald's, said Alison.

But I *want* to go to McDonald's, Rachel whined.

No, said Alison. She shot Chris a warning glance.

Chris kneeled in front of their daughter. Why don't you go play in your room for a little bit and then I'll come get you? he offered. Rachel gave Alison a withering glance and then did as Chris suggested.

Alison pulled the wine bottle from the fridge and poured herself a glass, then held a Corona out toward Chris. It was from the same six-pack he'd been drinking from the night he'd told her about Didi, she realized as he accepted it. Three-month-old beer. She hoped it made him sick.

Chris flipped off the cap, tossed the opener back into its drawer with a clatter, then downed a long swig. I don't want Rachel meeting every Tom, Dick, and Dickhead you bring home, he said.

This is the first time—

It won't be the last. I won't have it.

So what do you call it when she stays with you and Didi, huh? How is *that* different?

Didi and I are getting married, that's how. As soon as our divorce is final.

Alison rocked back on her heels, felt the sore ankle twinge. You *are*?

To Alison's surprise, Chris hung his head. She's pregnant.

Alison burst out laughing.

It's not funny, said Chris.

Oh, but it *is* funny, said Alison. Not quite the little love nest you pictured, is it? And baby makes three.

Fuck you, Alison.

Alison continued to laugh.

Stop it, Alison. I mean it.

Alison finished the wine in her glass and poured herself more. You know what *I* think?

I don't *care* what you think.

Well, here you are, so listen up. I think you wish you'd never left.

You do a pretty good job of convincing me I'm glad I did every time I'm here, said Chris.

Alison drank down the second glass of wine and emptied what was left in the bottle into her glass, then threw the bottle away. A little more won't hurt, she thought, taking another long sip. You can't tell me what to do anymore, Chris. That's what I'm telling you. If I want to have a friend over—a *male* friend over—I *will.* And I *can,* do you understand that?

We'll see, said Chris. He finished the beer and opened the cupboard under the sink, dropping his bottle with a loud thunk against Alison's empty wine bottle. Then he walked to the fridge and took the last bottle from the six-pack, retrieved the opener from the drawer and flipped off the cap. It clattered onto the cupboard, tottered, and then lay still.

Alison took another deep breath. We don't have to fight anymore, Chris. We can be friends. We can do what's best for Rachel—

That's what I'm *talking* about, Chris interrupted. You having that guy here—he gestured toward the living room with his chin, as if Sherman were still there—that's not what's best for Rachel.

You don't even know him, Alison said.

I didn't like him. He didn't *feel* right.

Alison laughed. Oh, are you Mr. Intuition now?

Chris downed a long swallow of beer. You'd better stop that, Alison.

He didn't *feel* right. Come *on*, Chris.

Chris leaned toward her across the kitchen island. I'd watch it, if I were you.

Alison drained the wine from her glass. You can't hurt me anymore, she said.

Chris stood. I can— Hi, Rache.

Can we go to McDonald's now?

In a little while, Alison said. Daddy and I are still talking. As soon as she'd said it she realized she had contradicted herself.

She could tell by her daughter's face that Rachel realized it, too. Okay, Rachel said. Then she ran out of the kitchen before Alison could say anything else.

In the kitchen Mommy and Daddy yell at each other and then Sherman says it is time for him to leave. You don't have to, Rachel tells him, but he says that yes he does. His sister is expecting him for dinner. Will you come back? Rachel asks him.

Sherman reaches over and takes her hand. You are my favorite girl, he says. I will always come back for you.

Okay, Rachel says, but then after he goes, she wonders if he ever really will. She remembers how Daddy told her the same thing once upon a time but Daddy lives with Didi now and only comes back to fight with Mommy. That is what they are doing in the kitchen now so Rachel goes there too because—well, just because. Daddy says he will take Rachel to McDonald's but Mommy says no. But if Daddy takes Rachel to McDonald's then they will have to stop fighting so when Daddy tells Rachel to go her room and then they can go to McDonald's she does. She tries to play with the Barbies but mostly she just listens to Mommy and Daddy yell. She can see herself in the patio door like it is a mirror, so she turns around and faces the other way.

After a while her tummy says it is *very* hungry, so she goes back to the kitchen again. You can't hurt me anymore, Mommy says, and Daddy starts to say something but then he sees Rachel and he stops. Hi Rache, he says. Can we go to McDonald's now? Rachel asks him. Instead of Daddy, Mommy answers. In a little while, she says, so Rachel hurries back to her room before Mommy knows she said something different from what she said before.

Outside now, Rachel can hear dogs barking: Bandit next door, and Carlotta next to Suzy Charles's house. She hears other dogs too, and then something else that is not a dog, so she opens up her patio door to hear better. The other sound is what is making the dogs bark. Rachel knows that because it makes a scary noise like Halloween, and the dogs answer, over and over and over. The scary noise makes her skin feel funny, hot and cold at the same time, and she feels funny in her ears, too, but maybe it is a good funny, she isn't sure.

The scary noise comes closer and the dogs bark faster and faster, especially Carlotta, who is a little dog and always makes a lot of noise. That Carlotta, Mommy always says. I wish she'd shut up. Rachel goes outside because she wants to see where the scary noise is coming from, and she climbs up on the chair on the patio and looks over the wall.

And there, sitting right in the middle of her street, is Chris, her coyote! His head is way back and his mouth is way open and out of his mouth is coming the scary noise, only it is not scary anymore. It is like wind and crying and water running all together. Chris! Rachel calls him. Here I am! But Chris doesn't hear her. He is too busy making his noise while Bandit and Carlotta bark and bark as if they are talking to Chris and he is answering them.

thirteen

PROTECT YOUR FAMILY AND YOUR ANIMALS!

Don't feed a coyote.

Don't pet a coyote.

Don't run from a coyote.

Don't leave pets or other small animals out at night without protection.

To the editor:

A great Sioux chief once said, "Great contentment comes with the feeling of friendship and kinship with the living things about you. The white man seems to look upon all animal life as enemies, while we look upon them as friends and benefactors." More famously, Chief Joseph said, "I will fight no more forever." It seems to me we should heed the words of those who were here first. There is much wisdom to be found there.

Peace,

Redfern Goldstein

To the editor:

First, we have Mrs. Harold and her New York ideas, like "sharing our space" with coyotes. Now we got another New Yorker, quoting Indians like they didn't make a mess of what they had. These easterners got a history of going where they aren't wanted and then pushing their way in. Well, listen up, girls. That won't happen here in Valle Bosque. The ways we got of doing things worked just fine before you got here, and they'll work just fine after you're gone. Now would be a good time to go, if you get my drift.

Jim Curtis

To the editor:

I'm from Buffalo, not New York City, and I find Mr. Curtis's thinly veiled threats insulting. Despite Mr. Curtis's assertion to the contrary, in this country people can voice their opinions freely, without threat of reprisal. Coyotes, unfortunately, cannot, which is why I (and, I imagine, Ms. Harold, too) have chosen to speak for them. Native Americans understand the value of peaceful coexistence. It seems many American men wouldn't know peaceful coexistence if it crept up and snuggled in beside them.

Peace,

Redfern Goldstein

To the editor:

Personal attacks won't serve any purpose but to deflect us from our stated goal of seeking solutions to the coyote problem here in Valle Bosque. Both Ms. Goldstein's contributions of Native American lore and Mr. Curtis's reminders of how longtime Valle Bosqueleños have dealt with the problem in the past are important aspects of our ongoing dialogue. Like Professor Putnam, I am hopeful that such a dialogue will ultimately suggest solutions. I implore all those involved to refrain from personal attacks and focus on our common dilemma.

Sincerely,

Natalie Harold

To the editor:

I had to laugh when I saw those letters from those New Yorkers. It reminded me of this book my wife was reading a while back about men from Mars and women from Venus. When I asked her what it was about, she said I wouldn't understand so why bother trying. I guess I don't understand what these other gals are saying, either. And I don't see why we should try to fix something that ain't broke. Coyote kills a chicken, man kills a coyote. Simple, straightforward. No one's come up with a better solution that I can see. Still, I'm listening. Maybe another man *can set me straight.*

Jim Curtis

To the editor:

I'm not someone who writes letters to the editor, but from what I've seen, not many of the people who write to the Valle Bosque Beacon *are. Jim Curtis's letter got me thinking. I'm sure not the smartest guy around, but I figure if someone will just sit here and listen to what everyone else is saying without going off half-cocked themselves, maybe we can begin to figure out the best thing to do. I guess I'm kind of electing myself, since no one else seems to have stepped up to the plate.*

Why me? Well, my wife always says I got a way of looking at things that's different from other people, and now a friend of mine has said the same thing. So I guess if everyone will just keep writing their letters— you, Jim Curtis, and you, Miss Goldstein and Mrs. Harold, and Professor Putnam and Mrs. Crawford, all of you, and then other folks, too—I'm reading them, and I'm thinking about what you're saying, and I'll bet other people are, too. I never figured it did much good to rehash what we already know or point fingers about what we already did. The way I fix something that's broke is to be smarter than whatever it is I'm fixing, and that's what I aim to do here.

I'm not promising anything. But I'll try. That's all I'm saying. I'll try.

Sincerely,

Anonymous Village Employee

Editor's Note: The letter writer asked that he not be named to protect his job.

When she heard Sherman come in, Natalie was in her study, finishing up her letter to the editor of the *Valle Bosque Beacon* about the coyote she'd seen on the ditch bank. She had decided she'd not send it right away; it was very different from her prior letters, and she wanted to read it over again in the morning before she did.

She wanted to tell Sherman about the coyote, but by the time she stopped typing, she could hear the modem sound that suggested he'd taken his laptop into the kitchen to check his email. Natalie reread what she'd written so far.

To the editor:

This afternoon as I was walking along the ditch bank, a coyote suddenly appeared, walking toward me. In its mouth, it carried a small animal, something recently killed but nonetheless indeterminate as to what it might have been. It may surprise Valle Bosque Beacon *readers to learn that this is the first time I have seen such a thing. But it's true: Until today, my knowledge of coyotes has been acquired through reading and information others have shared. Perhaps I am rare among Valle Bosqueleños; perhaps most have already encountered a coyote carrying its kill. This would go some way toward explaining certain attitudes so prevalent in this letters forum. I must say that after my encounter, I do think I have a better understanding of these attitudes.*

This is because what I felt when the coyote appeared was the most palpable terror I have ever experienced. I was riveted in place. I could not move, speak, nor even think about what I might do. When the coyote growled, though, I suddenly remembered that I was still holding a stick I'd recently picked up to examine some scat along the ditch bank. When I waved this stick in the coyote's direction, it disappeared as quickly as it had appeared.

A few minutes after my encounter, I suddenly vomited at the side of the ditch bank. A kindly man walking his dog inquired as to my well-being, and I thank him for his concern, which I did not have the presence of mind to do at the time. I don't know why I vomited. I mention it mainly because this episode, whatever its cause, seemed a direct result of my coyote encounter, and so a catalyst toward a reexamination of my beliefs regarding Canis latrans.

I know there are those in our village who believe I romanticize the coyote, but they both misunderstand me and mistake my motives. I neither champion the coyote nor defend it; I simply wish to make others aware that it, too, lives here in Valle Bosque. What I am trying to ascertain now is if this brief encounter has changed how I feel about our coexistence and my efforts toward educating Valle Bosque's citizenry. So far, my answer is that I feel more strongly about that education than ever.

I in fact wish that despite what I have said many times in this column, I myself had been better equipped to diminish my own fear, as well as the coyote's (because surely fear is why it growled at me), during my encounter. Having tasted such fear myself now, I believe that it is without a doubt what motivates those who campaign for the coyote's demise. But while I may understand that fear more clearly, I find I still cannot agree with their conclusion.

No matter how much their existence may terrify us, coyotes serve an important purpose. To name but one, they keep our rabbit population down, so that we may enjoy desert gardens that are not chewed to sticks in the night. Imagine how many rabbits would overrun Valle Bosque without the coyotes to control them.

But, you may say, what about the domestic animals coyotes eat? Indeed, this is the heart of our ongoing coyote debate here in Valle Bosque: the right of those who raise domestic animals versus the right of a wild creature. The right of a wild creature? *Farmers will likely laugh at my phrasing. But even after my encounter on the ditch bank, as horrific as it was for me (and, I suspect, for the coyote), I was left with a feeling of awe and gratitude to have seen this animal in the midst of what is most natural to it. Even if it* was *a domestic animal that coyote carried, it was only because the coyote had done what it does best.*

So my answer as to whether my attitude toward

coexistence with coyotes has changed is no; it has not changed at all. What has changed is my up until now "mild-mannered" approach to the problem. Where before I have sought to mediate, I will now seek to advocate. Where before I did my best to understand why someone like Mr. Curtis might want to shoot a coyote, I will now actively work to assure that Mr. Curtis never raises a gun toward a coyote again.

To that end, I have already left a message with a wildlife biologist from UNM who has been helpful in the past, in order to learn still more about (a) what humans may do when they encounter a coyote; and (b) what humans may do to deter coyotes from killing their domestic animals. I will share my findings via this letters column, as always.

Perhaps most important, though, I want to say how grateful I am to have had this encounter. It is one thing to admire the natural order of things academically. It is quite another to encounter it firsthand. It is my heartfelt wish that Mr. Curtis and others like him will come to understand this.

Sincerely,

Natalie Harold

Natalie saved and closed the document, then shut down her computer for the night. From the kitchen, she could hear the tap-tap-tap of Sherman's laptop as he responded to an email. To whom was he writing? And what was he saying? For the first time, Natalie wondered about the aspects of her brother's life she did not know. While she had always been forthcoming to Sherman, he'd been far less revelatory with her. Oh yes, he always *appeared* to be open and honest with her, but there were surely many things he'd never told her.

But why did that matter? Natalie took down the picture of Sherman, her parents, and herself that sat on the bookshelf above her desk. Sixteen-year-old Sherman gave the photographer an easy smile. Their parents' smiles were more strained, but, as they'd soon learn, their mother had lung cancer and their father a heart arrhythmia. Within the next five years, both would be gone.

From her allotted space in the photograph, seventeen-year-old Natalie met fifty-one-year-old Natalie's appraisal both seriously and guilelessly, but she wasn't really looking beyond the picture. No. She was looking at her smiling brother, at the passport *he* offered out of that picture and into the world. How could that young girl have been so trusting? Natalie wondered now. The world had seemed to her a book she might walk into and inhabit, a plot she might enter, a place she might belong. That Natalie had believed far-more-outgoing Sherman would be her guide and her protector.

And didn't she still believe that she could stay here safely, in her home in Valle Bosque, and have the world come to her? Not just via Sherman, either: Hadn't she sat all those years, waiting for a coyote to appear in her picture window? But it had only been when she had finally ventured out beyond her own well-delineated borders that a coyote—no, two coyotes—had shown itself, and she'd done so without Sherman to lead her. In fact, if she considered her day in its broadest context, she'd ventured out *despite* Sherman.

You still have that old picture?

Natalie looked up. She wasn't sure how long Sherman had been standing there, but she didn't ask him. She didn't answer him, either. She just set the picture back up on the shelf. She didn't even ask him what he'd done all day. Because what she'd done that day suddenly mattered to her far more than anything Sherman had ever done, would ever say, or could ever conjure. With a conviction she hadn't felt since she'd been the seventeen-year-old girl in the picture, Natalie knew that Sherman had never filled the role she'd assigned him in her life. It had been her all along. It had taken a coyote—and the most unlikely companion imaginable—to help her see that she was her own best guide.

Does she always see you drinking like this? Chris asked Alison. His glance still rested on the hallway Rachel had vacated, as if he could conjure her back.

I don't drink like this, Alison lied. You bring it out in me.

Chris swigged his beer. Yeah, blame me. Go ahead. Blame me for everything. Like you always do.

Alison toyed with her wine glass. She had been about to open another bottle, but she wouldn't, now. She wished Chris would just go, but that would leave her alone again, a prospect she had always dreaded almost as much as that of her and Chris continuing to sling words back and forth, the pointless and raucous jabber of magpies. There wasn't much hope of derailing their argument. At best, it would run itself in circles until its engine gave out, leaving a hollow silence more uncomfortable than the words themselves.

Chris finished his beer and set the bottle onto the counter with a loud clunk. He was waiting for her to say something, she knew. That was the nature of their arguments; bait and run, run and bait. Alison suddenly felt very tired. She was tired of Chris, tired of being there for Rachel when she was tired herself, tired of being tired. All she really wanted, she thought, was to be left alone. She'd never wanted it before, but she wanted it so badly now, she could feel its taunting lure just beyond her reach.

You were going to take Rachel to McDonald's, she said.

That okay with you? Chris asked. Alison looked up, surprised. It occurred to her that he might be tired, too. Maybe he was as tired of her as she was of him. If so, it was a new thing between them, this tiredness, an admission of defeat neither had been willing to concede before.

Just go, said Alison. She waved her hand in dismissal.

Chris bowed in mock submission, a last dig before he left the kitchen. Alison sighed at his departure. She'd have an hour to herself, she thought, an hour in which she might recapture something of the feeling she'd had during and after her bath. It seemed such a long time ago, that bath. Alison thought of Sherman Gold. Whatever had sparked between them was ash. She could feel the dull emptiness where her hope had resided.

Alison looked up. Chris was back. Rachel's gone, he said.

What Alison would remember later was the way her mind decelerated, or so it felt, while her chest constricted around her heart until all that was left was a stone clutched in the center of her. I have felt this way before, she thought, and recently. Her mind went at once to the coyote, the one that Rachel had named Chris. Then she realized that a coyote's howling had been providing background music for at least the last fifteen minutes. She strained to hear it now. It wasn't there.

Alison thought all this in the space of a heartbeat. Then she stood so quickly her stool clattered to the floor. The coyote, she said. She raced to the front door, flung it open, left it ajar. She darted barefoot into the dark night. She heard Chris behind her, shouting something. She couldn't hear the words.

Rachel! she called into the darkness. Carlotta, the neighbor's Chihuahua, yipped a staccato reply. Rachel! Alison ran into the cul-de-sac, stopped, called again.

Rachel! Chris called. Alison darted off again, running barefoot toward the subdivision's main road. Behind her, she could hear Chris's panting recede; he was trying to keep up, but must be dropping farther and farther behind.

Rachel! Alison called. At the sound, a deep-voiced dog joined Carlotta's refrain, and then another, mid-range. If Rachel answered her now, Alison thought, she wouldn't hear. She'd have to stop calling to quiet the dogs. And she'd have to stop running so she could listen instead.

She slowed to a walk and then stopped entirely. She felt her ankle twinge, shifted her weight to the other foot. Chris came up beside her, breathing heavily. Shh, she said, and he seemed to make an effort to quiet his breathing.

Do you hear something? he whispered.

Shh, she said again. I'm trying to listen.

Chris stepped away from her. They were standing in the middle of the intersection of two eerily quiet streets. At this far end of the subdivision, it was possible to believe that no one lived here. Cars were tucked into garages. People were hidden behind their adobe walls. Even the wind hung motionless in the blue wash of night.

One at a time, the dogs dropped out of their chorus. The last to stop was Carlotta. In the quiet that was left, Alison forced her hearing to adjust, to begin to hear the sounds in the silence. She knew they were there. And she knew that if she listened hard enough, she would hear Rachel, wherever she was.

Do you think the coyote—? Chris began.

Shh, Alison said. His words clattered to the asphalt and were gone.

Alison listened. First, she became aware of the hush of the air, the way it whispered with a voice all its own. Then, beneath that, she began to hear the sibilance of night lizards scuttling beneath the chamisa, a shushing sound not unlike her own *shh*.

Alison listened. Now she could hear rabbits, whispering through the sage. Snakes slithered long S's across the sand. Desert thrushes brushed against branches as they settled in for sleep. Even the antic ants could be heard if she strained hard enough, their industry an insult to the hour.

Alison listened. Above her, pinpricks of stars sang in the sapphire sky, whispers of cloud briefly skirting them before flitting on. Alison closed her eyes to the night to tune her ears more acutely.

Alison listened. Then she heard it: a whimpering. Her eyes flew open. She turned toward the sound. Listened again, then dashed through the sage in the direction from which it had come, the soles of her bare feet screaming a protest she ignored.

Behind her, Alison could hear Chris's loafers slipping through the dirt. Did you hear her? he demanded. Alison didn't answer. Crystalline grit lodged between her toes. Desert-dried weeds pricked her soles. Alison's ankle throbbed. Still she ran. She wanted to call, but she didn't. She ran toward the whimpering, closing the gap between herself and Rachel as if doing so would erase everything that had ever come between them.

When Alison got to the sound, her braking was cartoonish, Roadrunner at the edge of a cliff. Rachel sat cross-legged in the dirt beneath a chamisa, her cheeks smeared black with tears, a naked Barbie splay-armed in her lap. Alison squatted and pulled Rachel to her in one motion, then held her so as never to lose her again. She felt Rachel squirm in her grasp with a burgeoning of joy not unlike the very moment when Rachel had been born.

Chris runned away, Rachel cried. I tried and tried to catch him, but he just runned and runned. He is never coming back.

Ran away, Alison whispered. Chris *ran* away.

Panting heavily, Chris the father arrived. He squatted next to Alison. What happened? he demanded. He reached a tentative hand toward Rachel's head, then stopped it before it arrived. His hand wavered in the air, powerless and inconsequential.

Alison waited for Rachel to answer, then felt her

daughter shake her head against her chest, once, left to right. It's all right now, Alison said to Chris. Still holding Rachel, she stood, amazed at her own strength. Rachel wrapped her legs around Alison's waist, leaned her cheek against Alison's shoulder.

Can we go home now? she asked Alison.

Yes, Swee'pea. We can go home now. Alison started back through the field, her torn feet moving slowly, feeling every prick and barb as if it were a promise.

I can carry her, she heard Chris say behind her.

Alison didn't answer him. Holding tightly to her daughter, she tiptoed gingerly toward home.

Sherman wasn't listening, Natalie could tell. She'd stopped talking to get his attention, but he continued to stare toward the mountain, his thoughts somewhere far, far beyond it—or perhaps, Natalie thought, much, much closer.

She'd been telling him about the coyote. She had been wondering aloud at what it might have been carrying and had thought of the lop-eared rabbits she'd once seen at the State Fair. But when she'd asked Sherman what he thought, he hadn't answered.

Natalie had always valued how Sherman didn't invade her solitude, so she was surprised to realize how much she resented his departure now. She wanted to shake him, to say, I need to talk to you. Listen.

But that wasn't what she and Sherman were about. To change the rules now, when they were both well into middle age, wasn't a possibility. Natalie was the one who would always be there; Sherman would always be the one who came when he needed someone. That was the equation. Natalie couldn't suddenly say, I need you. Sherman wouldn't know how to be needed.

Natalie looked out the window. The night was full-dark now, the moon not yet risen. Through the chimney, she could hear a distant coyote, singing its singular song. Was it the same one she'd seen on the ditch bank? How many coyotes were left in Valle Bosque, she wondered, between Jim Curtis's shotgun and Ralph Sandoval's forced evictions? How much longer would she be able to sit here in her dining room, listening to a coyote's cry?

She thought again of the coyote on the ditch bank. Its coat had still been winter grey, patchy and mottled. Its yellow eyes spelled danger and wariness; the low growl was mere emphasis. What would Ralph Sandoval have done in her place? Natalie wondered. Would he have stomped his foot to make the coyote run off? Raised his arms, made a loud noise? Natalie thought that anything she learned from the UNM wildlife biologist she'd take to Ralph for examination. It was one thing to draw one's conclusions from books, after all; it was another to draw them from living one's life.

She had considered several times since getting home calling Ralph, and she considered it again now. She was hesitating because she'd never called him at home. She was also hesitating because she could feel what Ralph had said was that feeling like when you think you heard a mouse in the wall. Maybe there was something more, too. Maybe she knew that once she did call Ralph, something was going to change. Maybe she wanted to savor the status quo, however unsatisfactory it had become, just a little bit longer. *The devil you know*, Natalie thought, then looked sharply at her brother's face.

Sherman looked back at her, gave her a sheepish smile. Oh God, Nat. I am so sorry.

It's all right, Natalie said. Without another word, she returned to her study and closed the door. Then, before she could change her mind, she looked up Ralph Sandoval's phone number, punched it in, and took a deep breath that she held until Ralph answered.

Hi, she said.

Hey, said Ralph. I was just telling Nina how our boy ran.

Mommy carries Rachel to her room and lies her down on her bed and then she pushes the hair off Rachel's face and holds her hand there. She just looks and looks at Rachel but she is not mad, Rachel can tell.

Daddy stands in the doorway. Rachel can see the shape of him and the light from the hall behind him, but she can't see Daddy, not really. Daddy doesn't say anything either. Everybody is as quiet as naptime, as quiet as Chris when he saw Rachel and then he runned away.

Daddy makes a little coughing noise and Mommy looks up like she's surprised he is there. I guess I'll go, Daddy says.

All right, says Mommy. Rachel can hear that there is no more fighting in her voice, but it is not like she is giving up, it is more like she is the boss of him now, and whatever she tells him he will do.

I'll call you in the morning, Daddy says.

Don't, says Mommy.

Look— Daddy says.

Don't, Mommy says again.

Daddy's shape in the doorway changes, but he stands there some more before he goes out of the light. Then he comes to Rachel's bed and leans over and kisses her on the forehead. Goodnight, he says.

Sleep tight don't let the bedbugs bite, says Rachel.

All right, says Daddy, just like Mommy said to him. And then he just goes.

Rachel and Mommy listen to his truck start in the driveway and then Rachel listens to it drive away until she can't hear it anymore. Mommy listens longer and then she says, You ready for bed, Swee'Pea?

Rachel thinks that she has not had her dinner, but she decides that she is not very hungry anyway. She feels like something is different about Mommy and different about herself and different about Mommy and herself together, and it feels like it is a good something even though she doesn't know what it is. Will you read to me? she asks Mommy. Will you read me *The Runaway Bunny*?

Mommy leans over and hugs her and doesn't let go, just like she did outside after Chris runned away and then Mommy found her. Rachel likes it but it makes her feel like she can't breathe so she wiggles until Mommy lets go. I will read you *The Runaway Bunny* over and over and over again, she says. I will read you *The Runaway Bunny* when you are in college. I will read you *The Runaway Bunny*—

Rachel gets up and goes to her bookshelf to get the book. She takes it back and hands it to Mommy. Will you read it tonight, though? she asks her.

Mommy shoves her fist across her cheek and then pulls Rachel into her lap. She reads how if the bunny runs away, the mommy will find her. And just like the runaway bunny, Rachel hopes that she won't and she is happy that she will.

In his sleep, he heard voices, a chorus of women sometimes differentiated and sometimes not. Some spoke wisdom and some spoke nonsense and some spoke words of love and later words of malice and spite. Some whispered and some yelled and some spoke not at all but merely touched him with their thoughts and then were gone.

Tonight as he slept he heard a woman's voice telling him that she could love him, if he would let her. Hearing this, he tossed to his side, but the voice continued. You are afraid to be loved, the voice said. Men think love is a chain. Love is not a chain. Love is a ribbon that can dance unfettered or be tied into a graceful bow.

Why are you haunting me? he asked the voice in his dream. He had tossed to the other side, but still the voice whispered on. Women speak, and men do not hear, the voice said. Men speak, and women listen, only to hear that the men's voices do not say anything they wish to hear. That is the difference.

The voice faded and was still. Then, in the dark canyon of his sleep, he heard another voice, a voice not woman or man, a voice that seemed to come from a place long left behind, a time forgotten or buried. The cry went on and on, and when it did not stop he realized that he was no longer sleeping and that the voice called outside the window where he slept in his sister's house.

He was not someone whose sleep was often disturbed nor was he someone who often remembered his dreams, but he remembered the dream from which he had been awakened. He remembered too the voice in the dream and heard now the one that called outside and in that way things have in the dark the two voices became one, the ancient howl in the night and the whisper of the woman in the dream and half-asleep he believed that if he listened, really listened, just this once, everything could change. And so he went to the window and cranked it open and the voice of the coyote slid into the bedroom and wound around the walls and lifted to the ceiling and puddled on the floor. The voice of the coyote went on and on and he cocked his head and listened, not thinking anything at all.

Then, behind him, Natalie said, Did it wake you? and he turned. Without her glasses, his sister looked younger, the Natalie he remembered from when they were children, when their lives still lay before them, unwritten, and in that same odd way of night-thoughts he believed for a moment that perhaps they *were* still young, that all that had happened was yet to be. Young Natalie stepped further into the room, came and joined him at the window, where he looked out into the opaque night. On and on the coyote sang, and Natalie cocked her head now, too, as Sherman had, as he did now again.

Everything else ceases to matter when I hear them sing, Natalie said. *Dayenu.*

Sherman looked at her, startled with the suddenly remembered word. It should suffice us, he translated from the Hebrew.

It should, said Natalie. But it never does. In the morning, the voices will be gone. In the morning, everything will look clear in the bright light of day and we won't remember how it felt to stand here in the dark, listening.

I will remember, Sherman said.

No, said Natalie. You won't. Then she turned and left the room.

Sherman turned back to the window. The singing had stopped. He strained his ears toward the silence, hoping to will it back, but it was gone. And so he closed the window and went back to bed, and in a moment he was once again asleep, undisturbed by voices or by dreams.

the end

Acknowledgments

The excerpt from Charles Wright's poem "Two Stories" is from *The World of Ten Thousand Things: Poems 1980-1990*. Used by permission of the author.

The quotes that begin chapters 4 and 5, the first epigraph, and the story of coyote and crow that appears in chapter 9 are from J. Frank Dobie's *The Voice of the Coyote*. ©Little, Brown and Company. Used by permission.

The quotes that begin chapter 6 and 7 are from Hope Ryden's *God's Dog*. Used by permission of the author.

The quotes that begin chapters 11 and 12 are from Laurence Pringle's *The Controversial Coyote: Predation, Politics, and Ecology*. Used by permission of the author.

The quotes that begin chapters 1, 2, 9, 10, and 13 appear, in slightly different form, in a brochure distributed by the

Village of Corrales Animal Control Division called "Co-Existing With Coyotes in the Village of Corrales" in April 2002.

Additional source material was provided by Todd Wilkinson's *The Track of the Coyote*. Used by permission of the author.

This is a work of fiction. Any resemblance to people living or dead is unintended. The village of Valle Bosque is fictional as well, which should quiet those who wonder at the many liberties taken with the geography of my own New Mexico village.

This work would not exist without the quiet inspiration and thoughtful reading provided by Susan Weiss, activist extraordinaire. The letters to the editor column of the bi-weekly *Corrales Comment*, published and edited by Jeff Radford, also inspired me in obvious and not-so-obvious ways.

Thanks, too, to treasured friend and most excellent editor Beth Hadas, faithful friend and awesome agent Anne Hawkins, thoughtful friends and sister writers Judy Fitzpatrick, Barbara Furr, and Ann Paden, dear daughter and fine friend Kaitlin Kushner, whose artwork graces the chapter epigraphs, and constant friends and sisters of my heart Joanie Luhman and Judy Villella. Thanks to Kevin McIlvoy, whose faith inspires me to do my very best, and to the fabulous people at UNM Press: Evelyn Schlatter, Managing Editor; Robyn Mundy, Book Designer; Maya Allen-Gallegos, Production and Design; Amanda Sutton, Publicist; Rachel Gibbs, Event Coordinator; Glenda Madden, Marketing Director; David Holtby, Associate Director; Adrianna Lopez, Advertising Manager; Nancy Woodard,

Promotions; Bob Arnold, Jeannie Dunham, Sheri Hozier, and Kay Marcotte, Sales Reps; Luther Wilson, Director; Stewart Marshall and the warehouse gang; Lynne Bluestein, Receptionist/Mastermind; and anyone I've somehow forgotten or inadvertently overlooked. And, as always, Bob.

Lisa Lenard-Cook
Corrales, New Mexico
January 2004

Lisa Lenard Cook *lives in Corrales,*
New Mexico. She has an M.F.A. from Vermont College. Dissonance,
her first novel, also available from the University of New Mexico Press,
won the Jim Sagel Prize for the Novel in 2001.

www.unmpress.com